"I have a s... said Thimo.

"I have a private practice in Leiden. I employ two nurses and one, Willi, is going to Australia to see her brother for a month or six weeks and I wondered if you would care to take over her job for that time."

"I can't speak Dutch," claimed Esmeralda.

"I daresay Loveday will help you there; you won't need more than a few routine phrases."

Her impulse was to say yes at once, but she was a practical girl and could see several snags.

"I've no uniform and where will I live?"

"Willi will let you borrow hers, and she has a very small house near my rooms."

She said contritely, "I'm sorry Mr. Bamstra, you've been so kind to me." She looked down at her plastered leg with the cotton sock pulled over the toes to keep them clean.

"Call me Thimo."

"Thimo, then, though I don't think I should."

"You find me too elderly?" His voice was bland.

"Of course not, but you are a senior consultant at the hospital and I'm your patient..."

"Then let us compromise; call me Thimo when we are out of hospital and away from consulting rooms."

Romance readers around the world will be saddened to note the passing of **Betty Neels** this past June. Her career spanned thirty years and she continued to write into her ninetieth year. To her millions of fans, Betty epitomized the romance writer, and yet she began writing almost by accident. She had retired from nursing, but her inquiring mind sought stimulation. Her new career was born when she heard a lady in Amsterdam bemoaning the lack of good romance novels. Betty's first book, *Sister Peters in Amsterdam,* was published in 1969, and she eventually completed 134 books. She was a wonderful person as well as a hugely talented writer, and she will be greatly missed. Her spirit will live on in all her works, including those soon to be published.

THE BEST *of*
BETTY NEELS
ESMERALDA

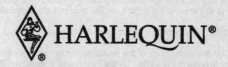

HARLEQUIN®

TORONTO • NEW YORK • LONDON
AMSTERDAM • PARIS • SYDNEY • HAMBURG
STOCKHOLM • ATHENS • TOKYO • MILAN • MADRID
PRAGUE • WARSAW • BUDAPEST • AUCKLAND

ISBN 0-373-63156-1

ESMERALDA

First North American Publication 2001

Copyright © 1984 by Betty Neels.

CHAPTER ONE

THE orthopaedic ward for children at Trent's Hospital was in the throes of its usual periodical upheaval: Sister Richards, on the edge of retirement, and, after a lifetime of caring for the small, sick children, a trifle eccentric, was making the cot change, an exercise which entailed her little charges being moved up and down the ward as well as from side to side, until none of them—and that included the nurses—knew exactly where they were any more, so that the children were either screaming with delight at being at the other end of the ward, or roaring with rage at being moved at all, and the nurses, especially those who were new to the experience, were on the edge of hysterics. And this time she had been fortunate in enlisting the help of the two housemen who had unwittingly arrived to write up their notes, and instead now found themselves, under Sister Richards' inspired direction, shifting cots too. One of them, trundling a cot containing a very small and cross girl, asked furiously: 'Is she out of her mind? Can't someone stop her? My notes…'

The girl he had addressed was guiding him towards the far corner of the ward. 'Certainly not,' she protested in a pleasant, cheerful voice, although it held a faintly admonishing note. 'It works splendidly, you know—the children are mostly here for weeks and they get bored; moving them round is good for them—they never know where they'll be next.'

'And nor do you, I'll be bound, Staff.'

'Well, it's a bit awkward at first, but we soon get sorted out.'

They pushed the cot into a corner, and he said: 'I do believe you like the old thing.'

'Yes, I do—and she's a wonderful nurse.'

He stood aside and watched her settle the small girl against her pillows, thinking that she seemed a nice little thing; not much to look at though; too small and thin, and all that mousey hair piled high—if it wasn't for her eyes she would be downright plain, but those green eyes, with their thick, dark lashes were really something. It was a pity about her foot, of course— he gave it a quick look and glanced away as she limped round the end of the cot. He was fairly new on the orthopaedic side and he had been warned about Staff Nurse Esmeralda Jones; she didn't take pitying glances easily, and anyone wanting to know, however tactfully, why it was that one small foot dragged so horribly behind its fellow would get a cold green stare and no answer at all. True, there was one person who could apparently say what he liked to her—the orthopaedic Registrar, Leslie Chapman. The young houseman had heard him boasting about it in the common room one day, and hadn't much liked him for it.

'Anyone else to shift?' he wanted to know cheerfully.

Esmeralda beamed at him. 'No thanks, you've been a Trojan. Sister will be having coffee in her office, I expect, and I'm sure she'll give you a cup—after all this, you'll be in her good books.'

He started to move away. 'What about you?'

She was adjusting a gallows frame with careful skill. 'Oh, I'll be along in a minute—it's Mr Peters' round in half an hour and this place looks like a fairground—we'll have to tidy it up a bit.'

She knew as she spoke that she would probably not get her coffee—even with three nurses to help her, it would take time to get the place straight, especially when half the children were objecting at the tops of their voices to being moved. She coaxed and scolded gently, slicked down untidy heads of hair, wiped faces and hands and then, with a minute or two to spare after all, was hurrying down the ward with the intention of swallowing a quick cup of coffee in the kitchen, when the ward doors were swung open—Mr Peters, bother the man, was early.

He was a short man, looking older than his forty years, and already going bald, which might be why he cultivated a heavy moustache and a formidable beard. The children loved him and the nurses went out of their way to fulfil his every whim. He stood just inside the doors now, bellowing good morning to the children, and added: 'Hullo, Esmeralda—taken you by surprise, have I?'

She fetched up in front of him, said 'Good morning, sir,' in an unflurried manner and added: 'I'll fetch Sister, she's in the office.'

'I know, I've been there—I thought you might like to know that I've brought someone with me. I've known him for years, we were students together—he's over here doing a few odd jobs, wanted to see the ward.' His eye roamed round his surroundings. 'Good lord, girl, Sister Richards' been having a moving day. Where's Benny?'

'Right at the other end, Mr Peters. Sister thought that he might like to see out into the inner yard.'

Mr Peters started up the ward. 'I'll say hullo to him while we're waiting,' he declared. 'You might as well come along too.'

Benny was his pet; he was everyone's pet as a matter of fact. He had come in weeks ago with a congenital dislocation of both hips, which was being painstakingly corrected by Mr Peters' skilled surgery, and beside having the appearance of an angel, he behaved like one too; he was never put out, grizzly or bored, and his Cockney sense of humour could be relied upon to cheer up anyone within range of his strident little voice, even on the gloomiest of days—but today was fine and warm, for it was almost midsummer, and he was sitting up in his bed, working away at a jigsaw puzzle which he immediately invited them to finish for him. They had obliged with one or two lucky attempts when the ward doors opened once more and the rest of Mr Peters' entourage spilled into the ward.

'Go and tell 'em to come up here, there's a good girl,' Mr Peters begged Esmeralda, and she set off across the shining parquet.

For some reason everyone had paused just inside the doors, so that she had the whole ward to walk down, and as always when there was someone she didn't know looking at her, she was conscious of her limp—more conscious than she need have been, too, she thought crossly; the man standing beside Sister Richards was staring at her as though she were exhibit A. She lifted her chin and stared back. He was something to stare at, she had to admit, tall and broad-shouldered and remarkably good-looking, with hair so fair that it was difficult to know if its fairness was silver. She looked away from his cool grey gaze as she reached them and addressed herself to Sister before attaching herself to the outer fringe of the party and going back up the ward once more. It was like Mr Peters to start in the middle of the round instead of at the first bed by the door like everyone else; Esmeralda received the little pile of folders from a harassed nurse and rearranged them quickly; it was too bad of Sister Richards to have had a moving day just before the consultant's round, and now there was no time to sort out the notes or the X-rays. She sighed, and using the foot of a cot as a desk, set to work to remedy that.

She had taken care not to send more than a fleeting glance in Leslie Chapman's direction, although she was well aware that he had been trying to catch her eye. How awful if their date for that evening had to be broken for some reason—their first, for though he had been unaccountably friendly towards her during the last week or two, it wasn't until the previous day that he had asked her out. She stacked the notes tidily, frowning a little; when Leslie had first joined Mr Peters' team, he had ignored her completely—worse, she had caught him eyeing her crippled foot once or twice with a kind of indifferent pity. And then one day he had stopped her in a corridor and asked some trivial question—she couldn't even remember what it had been any more, and after that he had shown a decided preference for her company, and when, rather shyly, she had asked him why he bothered to waste his time on a girl with a crippled foot, he had dismissed it airily, just as though it hadn't mattered at all, although he hadn't asked how it came to be crippled in the first place, and she, who was so touchy with anyone else who dared to ask her that question, found herself wishing that he would. Perhaps he might even know of someone who could perform a little miracle and turn her foot into a normal one again.

So many specialists had seen it and suggested first one thing and then the other, none of them the least use, so that for the last few years she had refused to have it looked at at all, even kind Mr Peters, when he had mentioned casually not so long ago that he thought he might have a solution, had received a firm refusal, and rather to her surprise, he had accepted it without demur.

She handed Mr Peters the notes he was asking for, caught Leslie's eye and smiled at him, and then stopped smiling rather abruptly because Mr Peters' old friend was watching her. She met his look for a moment and then turned away, wondering why he was there; not for consultation, evidently, for he had had little to say so far. True, he was nice with the children and his manner was pleasant and unassuming, but he was making no attempt to draw attention to himself. Probably he was paying a casual visit at Mr Peters' invitation, but she wasn't sure about that. He had an air of authority about him, and he was remarkably elegantly dressed for a GP; nothing off the peg—she peeped quickly as she looked for another set of notes; silk shirt, and unless her eyes were deceiving her, expensive shoes on his large feet.

She limped round the cot to prepare the occupant for Mr Peters' examination, taking care not to look at him again, although she found herself unwillingly wanting to know more about him. It seemed a little pointless to pursue this train of thought, though, for she wasn't likely to meet him again and it wasn't important.

But she was to meet him again; Mr Peters came back into the ward several hours later, just after Sister Richards had gone off duty, leaving Esmeralda with a list of jobs to be done, which, even if she had had twelve pairs of hands, she would have no hope of executing. She was toiling through the most tedious of them; arranging the written requests for holidays, days off and the like, so that her superior needed only to consult the neat list when she next made out the off duty, when the office door was opened and Mr Peters came in.

'Ah, not busy, I see,' he said; it was his usual greeting whatever the recipient of his attentions was doing, and Esmeralda, inured to constant interruptions, said politely: 'Oh, no, not in the least, sir. Did you want to see one of the children?'

'No, you.'

'Me?' she asked blankly. 'Whatever for?'

'What did you think of Mr Bamstra?' he wanted to know.

'That very big…your friend who came this morning? Well, I—I don't know—I didn't speak to him.' Anxious not to hurt his feelings, she added hastily: 'He looked very nice…' She was stuck there and finished lamely: 'The children seemed to like him—he got on well with them.'

'He gets on well with everyone. That foot of

yours—remember how the last time you allowed me to look at it, I told you that what it needed was someone who was a genius with a hammer, to smash the joints and then put them together again properly? Well, Bamstra does just that—half a dozen times so far, and each case a success. I asked him to come over and take a look at you.'

'You what?' She wasn't sure if she felt angry or excited or just disbelieving.

'Don't waste time pretending you didn't hear, Esmeralda, I'm a busy man.'

His tone implied that she was very much at fault and she found herself apologising as he said impatiently: 'Well, what do you say? He hasn't time to waste hanging around while you think about it—he'll want to talk to you and make certain that you've a good chance of a complete cure if he does operate. He seemed to think that he could do something from what he saw of you this morning.'

Esmeralda drew an indignant breath. 'So that's why you came into the ward first and went right to the other end, and then sent me all the way back with a message—so that he could watch me limp...' She choked with her feelings.

'That's it—how else was he to get a sight of you?' He added kindly: 'He wasn't looking at you, only casting a professional eye over your foot.'

'Well!' She had no breath left with which to be

indignant. 'And why, may I ask, am I singled out for his attention?'

'Because you're a nice girl and you've been taking it on the chin for years, and it's time that stopped or you'll turn into a frozen spinster.'

Esmeralda gave him an outraged look and he added quickly, 'No, on second thoughts you wouldn't, not with those eyes—my daughter has blue eyes, bless her, but I've always fancied green, myself.' And when she gave a chortle of laughter: 'I'll ask Mr Bamstra to come in.'

And before she could say another word, he slid through the door.

For a man of such massive proportions, Mr Bamstra was remarkably silent; he had taken Mr Peters' place while Esmeralda was still staring at the door. He said with a deceptive meekness which she didn't for one minute believe: 'Is it all right if I come in?'

She said vexedly: 'Well, but you are, aren't you? Sister left me with a great deal to see to, and I'm not even half way through it all.'

His smile was kind, it was also beguiling. 'You're put out,' he observed, his voice kind too, 'and I'm very much to blame, but it was a little difficult, you know. I could hardly drop in and say: "Oh, hullo, I've come to look at that foot of yours," could I?' He added more seriously. 'I didn't think you would want it mentioned until we had talked about it.' He sat down on a corner of the desk, looking down at her with intent grey eyes. 'You do want it put right, don't you?'

Her vexation had given way to a rather doubtful hope. 'Oh, more than anything in the world,' she assured him fervently. Her green eyes were full of dreams, although her voice was prosaic enough. 'A great many surgeons have seen it, you know, but just lately I've refused to let anyone see it.'

He pushed his large, well-kept hands into his pockets and studied his shoes. 'Tell me as briefly as you can just how it happened and what treatment you have had.'

He didn't look at her at all, which made it easier. 'I was three. I fell off my pony and he trod on my foot—nothing else was injured, just that foot; he crushed the metatarsals, pulped them into a squashy mess. The surgeon who saw it said he could do nothing then, that perhaps when I was older the bones would separate again and he could operate; only they didn't, they set themselves exactly as they were—they fused into a lump of bone. My mother took me to any number of specialists when I was a little girl, but none of them could do anything—they said that something should have been done when the accident happened. I've been to several other specialists since I started nursing, and they all thought that it had been left too late; that I would have to learn to live with it—that the limp didn't notice very much…'

'I noticed it,' said Mr Bamstra with a detached candour which didn't hurt at all. 'Shall I have a go?'

Her hands were clasped on her aproned lap, the fingers entwined so tightly that the knuckles showed white. There were no reasons to suppose that this man was any different from the others who had wanted to help her, and yet she felt no hesitation in saying yes: 'Only it might be a bit difficult. I mean, I'd have to get leave and all that—would it take long?'

'A couple of months, perhaps. Of course you would be in a walking plaster in no time, so you would be able to get about.' He stopped looking at his shoes and looked at her. 'Will you let me see what I can arrange? You would have to come to my hospital, you know.'

'Oh—where's that?'

'Holland—either Utrecht or Leiden, whichever has a bed for you.' He got off the desk. 'Think it over,' he advised her. 'I shall be here until tomorrow evening.' He nodded with casual friendliness and left her sitting at the desk, her head in a whirl.

But a look at the clock warned her that sitting and thinking about her own affairs was inadvisable; she couldn't hope to get finished before Sister Richards came back on duty, but at least she could get as much done as possible. She rushed through the rest of the requests and went down the corridor to check the clean linen, working with such a will that she was all but finished when Sister arrived. She went off duty herself an hour later, her head no longer full of Mr Bamstra's visit but of the evening ahead of her.

This was her first date for quite some time. Of course she went out often enough with the other nurses, frequently a bunch of them, together with housemen or students, made up a party, but although she was popular in a quiet way, no one had singled her out for an evening *à deux,* not that that surprised her in the least. If she were a young man, she wouldn't have bothered with a girl who couldn't dance, who couldn't even run for a bus without looking grotesque; she had no brothers of her own but she was aware that young men didn't like to be made conspicuous. Her mother and old Nanny Toms, who still lived at her home and did the housekeeping, had both assured her over and over again that when Mr Right came along her foot wouldn't matter to him at all, but here she was, all of twenty-six, and no one, let alone Mr Right, had even taken a second glance at her—not until now. Leslie Chapman's sudden attentions had taken her by surprise at first, but now, finally won over by his apparent desire for her company and his disregard for her limp, she was allowing herself to respond to him, and because her warm nature had been frustrated, hidden behind the matter-of-fact manner she had learned to assume against pity, it was threatening to take over from her hard-learned common sense.

She made her way to her room, refused the offer

of a cup of tea with a handful of off-duty friends, and opened her wardrobe door. Unlike many of the girls she worked with, she had plenty of clothes, pretty and quite often expensive, for again unlike them, there was no need for her to help at home. Her mother had been left comfortably off in the small manor house in the New Forest, and she herself had, over and above her salary, a generous allowance from the substantial capital her father had left for her. Only if she should marry before she was thirty would she come into full possession of her sizeable fortune, and in the meantime the fact that she was by way of being a minor heiress hadn't altered her independent nature in the slightest; she recognised that it was pleasant to have sufficient money to buy the things she wanted, but she had no highflown ideas about her inheritance and it said much for her nice nature that her friends, even if they were at times envious of her, never cast it in her teeth. And she, for her part, never mentioned it to them, nor, for that matter, did she mention the countless small acts of generosity she performed; the small sums she had lent and never wanted back, the countless times she had stood treat without anyone quite realizing it...she would have been horrified if anyone had found out.

She stood now, debating the merits of a pinafore dress in a soft pink with a white muslin blouse to go with it, or a green-patterned voile dress with a tucked bodice and short sleeves. She had no idea where they were going. Leslie had mentioned, rather vaguely, going out to eat; she had been a fool not to have asked him where. She chose the dress finally, if she wore her thin wool coat over it it would pass muster almost anywhere, and she hardly expected to go to Claridges or Quaglino's. She bathed and changed rapidly, slid her feet into pale shoes, wincing at the ugly built-up sole on one of them, matched them with a handbag and took a final look at herself in the looking glass. She supposed she looked as nice as she could; her mousey hair shone with brushing and she had coiled it smoothly on top of her head, although one or two tiny curls had broken free at the back of her neck. Her face was nicely made up, the dress was in excellent taste even if it was a little on the plain side, and she forced herself to take a matter-of-fact look at her feet. Standing very still with her crushed foot tucked behind the sound one, it hardly showed, but that was cheating. She brought it into full view and contemplated it in all its clumsiness.

She would have this operation Mr Bamstra had suggested, even if she had to go to the other side of the world and stay for months; Leslie liked her now, perhaps more than liked…surely if she had two good feet he might actually fall in love with her? She turned away from her image, rather defiantly sprayed Dioressence upon her person, and went down to the Nurses' Home entrance.

Leslie was waiting for her in his Lotus Elan, a

showy, rather elderly model with far too much chromework on it, and painted an aggressive yellow. Esmeralda didn't much care for it; her father had always driven a sober dark blue Rover, and her mother, since his death, had merely changed one model for another. She herself had a Mini which she drove rather well despite the drawback of her damaged foot, and that was a sober blue too, but this evening, with Leslie sitting behind the wheel smiling at her, she told herself that she was becoming stuffy in her tastes, even slightly priggish. She hurried towards him, quite forgetting her hideous limp.

He opened the car door for her, his eyes on her face, not on her foot, and at any other time Esmeralda might have asked herself with her usual common sense what there was about her ordinary features which should cause him to look so enrapt, but she had no common sense for the moment. She was spending the evening with one of the best looking young men in the hospital, and these emotions were going to her head like champagne, giving a glow and sparkle to her usual calm.

She got in beside him, scraping her lame foot over the door, and he winced, although when she looked at him he was smiling. 'You look charming,' he told her warmly. 'I thought we'd go to that Greek restaurant in Charlotte Street, if you would like that?'

Esmeralda said with all the eagerness of a happy child: 'Oh, yes, very much,' and then sat back while he drove through the hospital gates and joined the evening traffic. He was a showy driver, full of impatience and blaming everyone else except himself, but she wouldn't admit that, staying quiet until he pulled up with a squeal of brakes outside the restaurant.

It was a small pleasant place with candlelit tables and an intimate atmosphere. They decided on kebabs and Leslie made rather a thing about choosing the wine, so that Esmeralda felt a tiny prick of irritation deep under her pleasure, but she lost it once he had made his choice and settled down to entertain her, and presently, as they ate, he began to tell her of his hopes and ambitions. He had set his sights on a consulting practice, rooms in Harley Street and a pleasant house not too far away. 'It will be hard work,' he commented, laughing, 'but worth it if I have the right girl with me.' And he had looked at her in a way which quickened her breath.

'You'll need an attractive wife,' she told him, 'someone who can entertain for you and run your home and join in your pleasures—dancing...' She drank some wine and looked at him with a calm little face.

He moved restlessly in his chair, although he was smiling at her. 'There are other things than dancing.' He added: 'You're thinking about that foot of yours, aren't you? It's unimportant compared to a great many other things.'

She didn't stop to wonder what the other things might be; she said eagerly: 'Oh, don't you really mind? I'm used to it, of course, but it's not...' She smiled widely. 'That surgeon who came today—Mr Bamstra—he says he can cure it. He's already done several—he asked me to think about it.'

Leslie looked at her sharply. 'Did he indeed—he's a foreigner.'

She looked bewildered. 'Well, yes—Dutch. But nowadays people don't seem foreign any more, do they? I'll have it done...'

Her companion's eyes narrowed. 'You don't know anything about him—he might just be after your money.' And when she stared at him in surprise, he went on quickly: 'Probably he'll charge enormous fees and you'll have to borrow to pay him. I know what you nurses get—you'll be the rest of your life paying it back.' He smiled then. 'I only wish I could pay the fees for you.'

It was on the tip of her tongue to tell him that there was no need, that she could easily afford to pay him herself; that it had not, in fact, once entered her head, but something stopped her. She didn't think that he knew about her inheritance, for he had had no way of discovering it, and she wanted him most desperately to like her, for herself and no other reason—and if he did know, she would never be sure if it had been her money... His smile became tender, so that the doubts she had been harbouring melted away. All the same, she decided then and there to allow the Dutch surgeon to examine her foot. If Leslie liked her enough to take her out and not mind her awkward limp, surely if her foot were to be put right...? Esmeralda left the question unanswered.

CHAPTER TWO

ESMERALDA was doing the medicine round the next morning when Sister Richards sailed down the ward to her. 'It comes to something,' she complained crossly, 'when I'm forced to do my staff nurse's work while she dallies round with the surgeons—a foreigner, too.' She made it sound as though the visitor had horns and a forked tail. 'And you'd better not keep him waiting,' she added unexpectedly, 'he's one of those quiet men who explode when you least expect it.'

Esmeralda murmured suitably and hurried away, not caring about the limp for once. She didn't think that Mr Bamstra would explode, but as she hadn't had much experience of men, she couldn't be sure. She hurried on her own account; she had spent a wakeful night interspersed by dreams of a smitten Leslie completely won over, for as in dreams, not only had she two marvellous feet like everyone else, she had become quite beautiful too... She tried to clear her head of these ridiculous ideas as she went. Mr Bamstra wouldn't want to waste his time, he would expect clear answers to his questions, and somehow she must find the opportunity to ask him about fees.

Mr Bamstra was leaning his enormous bulk against Sister's desk, studying the off-duty book. He looked up as she went in, said 'Hullo,' in a friendly voice and then: 'What inconvenient off-duty you have!'

It wasn't at all what she had expected. 'Well, yes,' she said because she could think of nothing else on the spur of the moment.

He put the book down and studied her with a detached air. 'Have you decided to let me have a go?' he asked her placidly.

'Well, yes.'

'Good,' his voice was casual, 'I take it you have talked it over with someone or other—your parents?'

'Well…'

'Yes?' He smiled as he spoke and Esmeralda chuckled. 'I was going to say no,' she told him forthrightly. 'You see, Father's dead, and Mother has spent years trying to get my foot seen to—I thought I'd like to have it all arranged before I told her—she'll be wild with delight.' She added: 'And so shall I.'

'Ah—there is a young man, perhaps?'

She said seriously: 'Yes, at least I hope—I think so. He doesn't seem to mind that I'm a cripple, but it would be so much nicer…only he's not very keen on you doing it.'

Mr Bamstra studied the nails of his well-kept hands. 'He doesn't approve of surgeons?' His gentle voice would have coaxed words from a stone.

She spoke without thinking. 'Oh, but he's a sur-

geon himself. You met him yesterday—Leslie Chapman.'

Mr Bamstra, finding nothing wrong with his nails,
transferred his attention to his well-polished shoes.
'Ah—I am a foreigner,' he declared mildly. 'He
thinks I wouldn't be competent.'

Esmeralda was standing in front of him, her hands
clasped in front of her neat waist. 'He says you'll
charge enormous fees—that you are after my
money…'

He threw back his great head and roared with
laughter. 'And is that what you think too, young
lady?'

She eyed him impatiently. 'Of course not! You're
a successful surgeon—I expect your fees are huge,
but I don't suppose you need the money.' She added
reluctantly: 'Anyway, I can afford to pay them. Leslie
doesn't know that, though.'

Mr Bamstra made a small sound which he turned
into a cough. 'I—er—thought a nominal fee would
be in order. After all, the operation is still in its ex-
perimental stages—I daresay we might come to some
agreement about that; besides, we have a National
Health Service in Holland, too.' He got up from the
desk and strolled over to the window. 'Take off your
stockings or tights, or whatever it is you wear, and
let me see your foot.'

He examined the poor squashed thing with gentle
hands, and when he had finished said, more to himself

than to her: 'The middle metatarsals are flattened and fused, the last two pushed up and out of alignment—they'll need to be broken down, reset, and those two chiseled back into some sort of shape.' He set her foot gently on to the floor again. 'Why on earth didn't someone do something when it happened?'

'Well, I was only three, and Mother called in our doctor at once. He had it X-rayed at the local hospital and he felt sure that as the bones were still growing, they would right themselves. 'I—I was put to bed for a couple of weeks and then encouraged to walk. I had physiotherapy too.'

'Indeed?' The surgeon's face was inscrutable.

'And it got steadily worse?'

'Not straight away—it hurt for quite a while, just an ache, you know, and then it stopped hurting and I began to limp. Mother and Father took me to any number of specialists, and they all said that after so many years there was really nothing to be done.'

He nodded his head and took out a notebook and scrawled something in it. 'I'll see your matron—no, Principal Nursing Officer now, isn't it? I feel sure that something can be arranged—would you be prepared for whatever is suggested?'

Esmeralda said eagerly: 'Of course,' and felt quite disappointed when he walked to the door.

'I'll arrange for an X-ray,' he told her in such a vague voice that she felt sure that he was thinking

about something else. As he went through the door:
'I'll keep in touch.'

Which could mean anything, and so often were
words uttered by someone who was opting out… She
went back to her medicine trolley wondering when
she would see him again. If he was a very important
man, and he seemed to be, although he had given no
hint of that, it would probably be months before she
heard. She thanked Sister Richards, fighting a disappointment that was so strong that the muddled state
of her usually spick and span trolley caused her to do
no more than sigh perfunctorily.

She had put away her medicines and embarked on
the daily dressings when Sister Richards stalked up
the ward once more.

'X-Ray,' she said in tones of umbrage. 'You're to
go at once, Staff Nurse.' And then in quite a different
voice, letting Esmeralda see the motherliness which
only her little patients knew about: 'What's the matter, child? Is that foot of yours being a nuisance?'

'I was going to tell while we had coffee,' Esmeralda told her breathlessly, and poured it all out in an
excited spate of words.

'H'm—well, there's no knowing what that foreign
man can do, I suppose—the children like him, so I
suppose there's some good in him.' She reverted to
her usual brisk manner: 'Go along, Staff Nurse,
you're keeping them waiting.'

It was a pity that when Esmeralda returned to the

ward it was to find that Leslie had paid his morning visit and had gone again, now it wasn't likely that she would see him again that day. He had said nothing about seeing her again; nothing certain—although he had hinted that he hoped that their evening out would be one of many, and though he hadn't kissed her, he had held her hand for quite a long time. Esmeralda, who was old-fashioned and way behind the times in such matters, thought that that constituted quite a step forward. She spent the rest of the day in a rather dreamlike state, wondering about Leslie's real feelings towards her. She wondered about her feelings towards him too, for somewhere at the back of her mind was an uncertainty that the whole thing might be moonshine: she wasn't such a fool that she didn't realize that his interest in her might be fleeting and casual.

But something happened to change that; she was going off duty, her limp rather more pronounced than usual because she was tired, when Leslie caught up with her as she crossed the inner courtyard.

'So you've been X-rayed,' he remarked in an interested voice, and when she asked in surprise how he knew that: 'I was down there an hour ago, looking at Benny's last lot of X-rays, and I happened to see the report on yours. They're in a mighty hurry, aren't they? Getting the report out within a few hours— what's the haste?'

'I don't know, unless Mr Bamstra asked them to

be quick with it.' She glanced at her companion's face, but it looked unconcerned.

'You'll tell everyone, of course?' he wanted to know.

They had reached the Nurses' Home. 'Oh, yes— and it's my weekend, so I can go home.'

He smiled charmingly at her. 'Would it be an awful nerve if I offered to drive you? It's my weekend too.' He added softly: 'And I'm very anxious to know more about it and that you should do the right thing, Esmeralda.'

She stared up at him, trying to read his face. She asked bluntly: 'Would you be glad if my foot could be put right?' She took a deep breath. 'Why?'

'My dear girl, do I have to dot the I's and cross the T's? Of course I would be glad, although you are quite delightful as you are—still, if you've set your heart on it...' The smile came again. 'I must admit that a doctor's wife who can dance and play tennis and generally keep her social end up is a great asset.'

'Oh,' said Esmeralda, and then again: 'Oh—well, it would be very nice if you drove me home. You'd stay the night, wouldn't you?'

He masked triumph with another delightful smile. 'I'd like to very much—wouldn't it be inconvenient for your people, though?'

'Mother won't mind, and there's plenty of room— I'll telephone her tomorrow.'

He caught her hand briefly and gave it a squeeze,

and then because a small party of nurses had almost
reached them, said a brief goodbye and strode away.
Esmeralda, joining her companions, spent the evening
in a dream, from which she was impatiently roused
by her friends from time to time. 'Anyone would
think that you were in love,' declared Pat Sims, the
staff nurse on the Medical side and one of her closest
friends. Esmeralda longed to say 'I am' and dumb-
found them all, but she held her tongue.

They drove down to the New Forest on the Friday
evening—it had been a hot, sunny day and now the
warmth was tempered by a small breeze. Esmeralda,
in a cool cotton dress, sat contentedly beside Leslie,
hardly noticing his impatient driving, her thoughts already far ahead of her, wondering if her mother and
Nanny would like him, and what he would think of
her home. Once through the worst of the traffic, however, Leslie relaxed a little and laid himself out to
entertain her, and the journey passed quickly enough,
although she thought secretly that he drove a good
deal too fast, and felt relieved when they turned off
the A35 on to the open road which would lead them
to Burley. It was still light, but the sky had paled and
the road ribboned between rolling heath and patches
of forest, fading into twilight ahead.

'There are ponies,' she warned him. 'They roam
everywhere.'

'I know that,' he began impatiently, and then gave

an apologetic laugh. 'Sorry, I must be getting tired—that was quite a list we had this morning.'

Esmeralda was instantly sympathetic. 'And Mr Peters goes like the wind, doesn't he?'

Leslie grunted. 'That Dutchman was there—scrubbed too...showing off...'

She heard the malice in his voice. 'You don't like him.' She started and realized at that moment that she did.

'Oh, I wouldn't go as far as to say that. He's so damned sure of himself, though, just because he's perfected a method of correcting crushed bones—why, anyone could do that.'

'Then why haven't they?' she demanded sharply, 'And that's a beastly thing to say, for he's not here to defend himself.'

Leslie pulled the car savagely round the next bend and had to brake hard to avoid a pony in the middle of the road. He said grudgingly: 'Sorry again, I told you I was tired—perhaps I shouldn't have suggested bringing you.'

She protested warmly at that. 'And if you're tired, a day at home will be just the thing,' she assured him. 'Mother loves having people to visit her and Nanny will spoil you.'

But Nanny did no such thing. Esmeralda, getting ready for bed in her own pretty room, looked back on the evening with mixed feelings. Her mother had been delighted to see her; she always was, for they

were devoted to each other, and she had welcomed
Leslie with gracious friendliness. They had gone into
the low-ceilinged sitting room, with its oak beams and
beautiful furniture, and had drinks and Leslie had
looked about him and made just the right remarks
about everything. He had been impressed, and that
had pleased her; she loved her home, and his low
whistle of involuntary admiration and surprise as they
had approached the house had delighted her, for it
was indeed beautiful—not large, but perfect of its
kind and set in charming grounds of some size, and
he had been just as impressed when they went inside.

It was Nanny who had come to take him to his
room. She had entered the sitting room, a round, old-
fashioned, cosy woman, no longer so young; submit-
ted to Esmeralda's affectionate hugs with obvious
pleasure and had then said her how do you do's very
correctly, her sharp brown eyes taking in every inch
of the young man as she led him away.

It had been an hour later, while they had been waiting for her mother in the drawing room, that Leslie
had commented, half laughing: 'Your Nanny doesn't
like me, I fancy.'

Esmeralda had told him that Nanny quite often
didn't like people when she first met them, which was
fairly true but a little disturbing, for she had wanted
everyone to like him. She frowned as she got into the
little fourposter bed she had slept in all her life; she
wasn't quite sure about her mother either. Her parent

had been just as she always was, a delightful hostess, a pretty, middle-aged woman, thoughtful for her guest, prepared to entertain and be entertained, and yet there had been something... Esmeralda rearranged her pillows and frowned heavily in the dark.

It had been a pity that Leslie had made that remark about the silver in the display cabinet—lovely old stuff, worth a fortune, he had said, and although Esmeralda had seen no change in her mother's expression, she knew quite well that that lady was displeased, and he had made it worse by asking how many servants there were and if the house cost a lot to run. Her mother had answered him lightly without telling him anything at all, and turned the conversation with practised ease to himself and his work. He had made no secret of his ambition, and Esmeralda, defending him, saw nothing wrong in that—young surgeons who wanted to get on early in life, needed ambition to keep them going—only he had rather harped upon money, and she, fortunate to have been brought up in a home where money had been plentiful, and taught from her youth to be glad of it but never to boast of its possession, didn't quite understand his preoccupation with it. Her father, when he had been alive, had pointed out to her that having money, while pleasant, was by no means necessary for happiness. Leslie seemed to think that it was. She went to sleep thinking about it and woke in the morning with the thought still uppermost in her mind.

It was a gorgeous morning again. Esmeralda dragged on her dressing gown, stuck her feet into slippers and went along to her mother's room with the intention of sharing morning tea, a little habit they had formed after her father's death. Once curled up on the foot of her mother's bed, sipping her tea, Esmeralda plunged into the subject uppermost in her mind.

'Do you like Leslie, Mother?' She leaned across and took a biscuit.

Her parent eyed her fondly. 'He's a very attractive man, darling, and I'm sure he's clever—he should go far in his profession. Is he sweet on you?'

'Mother, how old-fashioned that sounds! I don't know—would you mind if he were?' She didn't give Mrs Jones time to reply but went on eagerly: 'You see, he doesn't mind about my foot, and if I had it put right...'

'Yes, dear, we must have a little talk about that—there wasn't much opportunity last night, was there? You've decided to have something done?'

'Do you think I should? It was all rather unexpected and I don't want to be rushed into anything—only this Mr Bamstra...'

'Such a nice man,' interpolated her mother unexpectedly.

'Mother, you don't know him? How could you—you've never met.' Esmeralda turned bewildered green eyes on her mother's unconcerned face.

'I met him on Thursday; he came to see me about you—to explain about…no, dear, don't interrupt. I think it was very nice of him. Not every mother likes the idea of her daughter going off to another country, even if it is for an operation by an eminent surgeon.' She smiled suddenly. 'Pass your cup, love.'

She poured more tea while her daughter held her impatience in check. 'I like him,' said Mrs Jones at length, 'and so did Nanny; she gave him some of her cowslip wine, and you know what that means— what's more, he drank it like a man and complimented her on it in a nice sincere way, nothing fulsome.' She popped a lump of sugar into her mouth and crunched it. 'Nanny says he's Mr Right.'

'Mother!' exploded Esmeralda. 'He's years older— at least, I suppose he is—he must be married and have a horde of children. Besides, there's Leslie.'

'Yes, dear, that's what I told Nanny just now when she brought me my tea. What would you both like to do today? You don't need to go back to Trent's until tomorrow evening, do you?' She passed the rest of the biscuits to her daughter. 'What does Leslie think of this operation?'

'He isn't very keen—well, he wasn't at first. He doesn't like Mr Bamstra, although yesterday he said it might be a good idea…'

'A doctor's wife—a successful doctor's wife— would have a certain number of social duties,' mused her astute parent, 'naturally, it would be very much to your—and his—advantage if you had two pretty feet.' She paused. 'Do I sound heartless and flippant, darling? You know I'm not—if I could ever have that foot of yours, I would; I've never ceased to regret...''

Esmeralda bounced across the bed and put her arms round her mother's shoulders. 'Mother darling, you've always been a brick about it. If it hadn't been for you being so sane about it, I should have been a neurotic old maid by now. It was you who showed me how to live with it, and I do, you know—only now, with Leslie... I'd like to take a chance.'

'It won't be a chance; not with that nice man, it'll be a certainty.'

Esmeralda had thought vaguely that they might ride over the forest during the morning. She rode well herself—everyone did in that part of the country, although she didn't hunt; she had too much sympathy for the fox, but ambling around on her mare Daisy was something she enjoyed, and it surprised her, when she broached the subject at breakfast, to discover that Leslie didn't ride; what was more, he didn't like horses. She had noticed the previous evening that he had repelled the advances of Maudie and Bert, the elderly labradors, but she had excused him then on the grounds of him not knowing them, but now it was apparent that he didn't like animals very much. She suggested a walk instead and was instantly sorry, for he said at once in a concerned voice: 'Oh, my dear, no—not with that foot of yours.'

Nanny had been passing as she spoke and she had uttered the small tutting sound which Esmeralda remembered so well as a sign of her disapproval. She had given Nanny a green stare of anger; couldn't she see that Leslie was concerned for her comfort? She agreed readily enough after that to go in his car to Ringwood, where they wandered round the shops amongst the holidaymakers, an exercise far more tiring to her crippled foot than a morning's stroll in the forest. It was fortunate that after lunch Mrs Jones should suggest that they might go over to some friends a few miles away and swim in their pool. 'They told me to bring you over the next time you were home,' she declared, 'and it's a heavenly day. I'll take my car, shall I? I know the way.'

The friends lived in a Victorian villa of great size and ugliness but with plenty of ground around it. The pool was at the back of the house and already the younger members of the family were in it or lying around in long chairs at its edge. Swimming trunks were found for Leslie, and Esmeralda went off to change.

She knew everyone there; most of them since she had been a small girl. She dived neatly off the side and swam a length or two before going to the side to call Leslie. 'It's heavenly,' she cried, 'come on in!' And she swam off again, as smoothly as a seal, happily aware that however much she was hampered on dry land, in the water she was just about as good as she could be, so that his look of surprised admiration made her glow with happiness. The glow faded a little when she got out of the water and went to sit with the rest of them; no one took any notice of the grotesque little foot stretched out on the grass, no one save Leslie, who gave it a quick, furtive glance and looked away again, and then, as though fascinated, looked again. But his manner towards her didn't change; he was still charming and just a little possessive and full of praise for her swimming; the glow started up again, so that her lovely eyes sparkled and her cheeks pinkened, and when they went back home after tea she told her mother, quite truthfully, that she hadn't enjoyed herself so much for years.

She changed into one of the pretty dresses hanging in the fitted cupboard in her room and went along to her mother's room once more, to perch on the bed and watch that lady do her face.

'Mother, what did Mr Bamstra say?' she asked at length.

Her mother laid down her lipstick and turned to look at her. 'He told me exactly what he was going to do; he told me that he intended to arrange for you to go to Holland so that he could operate there—in his own theatre. He said that you would be walking, God willing, with all the grace of a princess—yes, he said that—in a matter of two months, and dancing like a fairy in three. He suggested that I might like to come over and see you, and of course I said yes.'

'That would be marvellous, but Mother dear, how am I to get leave to go?'

Her mother smiled. 'I think perhaps he has all that sorted out.' She turned back to her mirror. 'Your father would have liked him.' She added on an afterthought: 'He comes from Friesland, I suppose that's why he's so very outsize.'

She gave a final pat to her hair, mousey hair like her daughter's and only lightly streaked with grey. 'And now let's go downstairs and give that young man of yours a drink.'

The evening passed pleasantly and Leslie was so charming and such an entertaining companion that Esmeralda relaxed completely; her mother must surely see now just how super he was. She went to bed presently, feeling quite content with her world. Everything was going to come right after all; she wouldn't be a cripple any more, and Leslie would go on falling in love with her and they'd get married. She floated off to sleep on a dream, which, while quite impractical, was nevertheless most satisfying.

And nothing happened on Sunday to mar her satisfaction. They went to church in the morning, taking it for granted that Leslie would go with them, and when they got back Esmeralda went to the kitchen to help Nanny to get the lunch, just as she had always done, for Dora, Nanny's niece, had the day off on Sundays, and Mrs Pike, the daily help, never came at the weekends.

'He'll have to put up with cold,' said Nanny as soon as Esmeralda put her face round the door. 'There's soup and a raised pie I made yesterday, and one of my trifles.' Nanny, over the years, had turned out to be as good a cook as she had been a nanny. She thumped the pie down on the large scrubbed table in the middle of the kitchen and said rather crossly: 'You can make a potato salad, Miss Esmeralda, if you'd be so good.' She stirred her soup. 'Do you see much of this young man at the hospital?'

'Well, yes, Nanny—he's the registrar on the ward where I work, you know. I see him most days.'

'And after work too, I'll be bound.' Nanny's voice was sharp.

'Sometimes. Don't you like him, Nanny?' Esmeralda's voice was wistful although she didn't know it.

'Now, love, if he's the man for you and you want to marry him and he'll make you happy for the rest of your life, then I'll dote on him.' She bustled to the sink and turned on the taps with a great deal of vigour. 'I hear from your mother that you're going away to have that foot of yours seen to. I always knew that there was someone in the world who could put it right for you. It'll be a treat to see you dance—I only hope I live to see the day.'

Esmeralda put down the potato cutter she was busy with and went over to the sink. 'Nanny, what a thing to say! Why, you've always vowed that you'll be nanny to my babies even if you have to live to be a hundred.'

Nanny thumped a saucepan down hard. 'And it'll have to be a good deal sooner than that if I have my wish, and I will. You mark my words—Nanny's always right.'

And having uttered this familiar phrase, so often repeated during Esmeralda's childhood, she nodded her head, picked up her pie and told her erstwhile nursling to make haste with what she was doing.

Lunch was a gay meal and afterwards they sat in the garden, doing nothing much until Esmeralda went to get the tea, because on Sunday afternoons Nanny went into Burley to have tea with a friend and then go to church with her—and then it was time for them to drive back to London. When their goodbyes were said, Esmeralda was quick to notice that her mother didn't suggest that Leslie should come again, although she said in her sweet, rather vague way: 'I expect we shall see each other again, Leslie,' and added the motherly rider: 'And do be careful driving, won't you. You know what the Sunday evening traffic is at this time of year.'

He had carried their cases out to the car then, and Esmeralda had hugged her mother and seized the opportunity to say: 'I'm very happy—I really am. I'll be down again just as soon as I know what's happening next.'

'Do, darling. I had thought of doing a little shopping soon. We might manage an hour or two together while I'm in town. I'll only come up for the day, though—London's awful at this time of year.'

They smiled at each other with deep affection and Esmeralda got into the car. Leslie was already in it; he leaned across her and shut the door and waved a careless hand, but she waved until her mother was a speck on the porch before the door.

They stopped for dinner at Alton, and because the traffic had been thick on the road and there were still another fifty miles to go, Leslie was a little impatient. Esmeralda, who was hungry and had been looking forward to a leisurely meal at the Swan or Alton House, found herself eating a leathery omelette and refusing a pudding so that they could get on to the road again as soon as possible. But she was happy enough not to mind too much, and when they at length reached the hospital and Leslie dropped her off at the Nurses' Home and kissed her rather perfunctorily, she was more than content; she hadn't been kissed so many times that she was aware of its lack of warmth. She went up to her room, made a pot of tea, had a bath and got into bed, to fall asleep at once.

CHAPTER THREE

ESMERALDA didn't see Leslie during the whole of Monday; by the evening she was as cross as two sticks and her long-suffering friends were glad when she declared that she had a shocking headache and would go to bed early.

'Clever Boy hasn't been near her all day,' explained Pat. 'He's playing the poor poppet like a trout; he's after that money of hers, of course—it'll come in handy when he sets up in Harley Street, won't it?'

There was a general snort of indignation. 'Can't we warn her?' asked someone.

Pat shook her head. 'Esmeralda's a darling,' she said, 'still believes in fairies and being happy ever after and strong, silent heroes. She's also got a very nasty temper once it's aroused; she'd only throw everything in sight at us and do exactly what she wanted.' She paused to refill her mug from the teapot. 'But now I'll tell you something. You know Paddy, the new radiographer? Well, he told me that that foreign surgeon—old Peters' friend, isn't he?—asked for an X-ray of her foot. Now I wonder...'

Her friends drew a little closer. They were fond of

Esmeralda and the more worldly ones had a very shrewd idea of the registrar's plans—not that they had any objection to him marrying money if he wished to, but they didn't like the idea of him marrying Esmeralda in order to get it. 'And for heaven's sake,' said Pat, 'if this man's going to patch up her foot, let her have some fun with it before she settles down— and not with our Leslie. Now, not a word from any-one. She'll tell us when she's ready, bless her, and it'll be up to us to encourage her to have something done. Who knows, while she's away Clever Boy will probably find himself another heiress.'

Esmeralda went on duty the next morning in a de-cidedly touchy mood, divided between the hope that Leslie would surely pay his usual daily visit to the ward, and the determination to treat him with casual coolness. She didn't have long to wait before getting the chance to carry out her intentions; he came through the doors a few moments after Sister Richards had gone across to drink coffee with Sister Brown on Women's Surgical, and made straight for her as she went from cot to cot, charting the TPRs.

He said at once with an apologetic smile: 'Hullo— yesterday wasn't the same, not seeing you, but each time I started off to come here, I got held up.'

Esmeralda's green eyes were very bright; she had seen him on two separate occasions during Monday, being held up by two of the prettiest nurses... 'Oh? I had a busy day too, as a matter of fact. I'm busy now; Sister wants this done before she gets back.' She smiled nicely at him and hoped that the pleasure of seeing him didn't show too clearly on her face. It couldn't have done, because he was taken aback.

'I thought we might have had five minutes together in Sister's office,' he frowned. 'You're a bit scratchy, aren't you?'

No girl, however much in love, likes to be called scratchy by the object of her affections. Esmeralda frowned quite fiercely. 'I am…' she began stiffly, and stopped abruptly because the ward doors had been opened and Mr Bamstra was advancing towards them with his leisurely stride. He interrupted them without apology, bidding them good morning in a no-nonsense voice.

'If you could spare me five minutes of your time, Staff Nurse?' he enquired with the faintest hint of sarcasm. 'In Sister's office, I think—I have asked her permission to interrupt your work.' He bestowed a frosty smile upon the registrar and then turned his back on him, his eyebrows lifted. 'Now?' he queried gently. 'I am rather busy.'

She went down the ward with him, a little pink in the face, the built-up sole of her shoe sounding like thunder in her ears, but for once she didn't care, and when he asked: 'Did I interrupt something? I do hope not.' She said peevishly: 'Yes, you did—surely you could see…'

'Oh, dear, yes,' he assured her blandly. 'All your little patients could see too—were you quarrelling?'

They had reached the office door and he opened it and stood aside for her to stomp past him, then he shut the door quietly behind him and leaned against it, staring at her. 'Never mind—next time you meet him you will have forgotten what it was all about,' he told her kindly, and smiled. 'But much though I would like to, I have no time to advise you on your—er—affairs of the heart. No, don't interrupt me, I beg you, just listen to what I have to say and then I'll go. I've spoken to your Principal Nursing Officer and she suggests that the best thing for you to do is to resign as from now—you have three weeks' holiday due, I'm told, which means that you will be free to leave at the end of next week. When you are fit to work again, you will be re-engaged—about ten weeks' time, I should suppose, but we can't be too arbitrary about that at the moment. There will be a bed for you at Leiden and if you can arrange to come over on—let me see, today is Tuesday—Sunday week, I will see that you are met at Schiphol.'

He had his hand on the door, ready to leave. 'Get a single ticket,' he warned her, 'for you might wish to return by sea.' He actually had the door open when she managed to get a word in.

'You went to see Mother.'

'Ah, yes—it seemed to me that she should know a little about me and about the operation I propose to do on your foot. I had no opportunity of telling you,' he assured her suavely.

She choked with temper. 'I'm quite old enough to tell my mother myself!'

'Of course you are, but mothers are prone to worry about their children, aren't they? I might have been a charlatan, you know; convincing enough to have taken you in and charming enough to persuade you against your better judgement, as well as emptying your pockets. Now she is satisfied that I am merely a run-of-the-mill surgeon with a passion for straightening crooked bones.'

Esmeralda's bad temper had melted away, and she nodded her head like a small, obedient girl. 'Yes, of course,' she agreed, and smiled. 'Nanny liked you.'

'A mutual liking, I assure you.' He nodded briefly and went, leaving her with a dozen questions on her tongue and no one to answer them.

Most of them were dealt with by Miss Burden, whose summons to the office she obeyed half an hour later, and if she had had any doubts about the whole undertaking, that lady's calm acceptance of the situation put them completely at rest. 'Take your days off on Friday and Saturday of next week,' she commanded kindly. 'I will speak to Sister Richards—that will give you time to pack your things and go to your home. I understand from Mr Bamstra that you are to fly and that he recommends a late afternoon flight— he asked me to give you this telephone number so that you may let him know at what time you will arrive at Schiphol.' She smiled briefly. 'I daresay you are surprised that you have been asked to resign, Staff Nurse, but that seems to be the simplest way of doing things; as soon as you are pronounced fit for work again, you may apply for your post and I am sure that you will get it again without difficulty, but should you feel that you needed a quieter job, it leaves you free to take one. I should point out to you, however, that Sister Richards will be retiring soon and I have long considered you as Ward Sister in her place, but that is a matter to be discussed later. Whether Mr Bamstra will find you fit for light duties before you return here is entirely up to him.'

Esmeralda said: 'Yes, Miss Burden,' and thought privately that there were a great many loopholes in the scheme, but it was hardly her place to say so. People like Miss Burden seldom admitted to mistakes; to be fair, they seldom made them. She went back to the ward, her head filled with a nice jumble of what clothes to take with her, plans for a day at home before she left, and the resolve to give a party to her friends. Strangely enough, she had forgotten all about Leslie.

The rest of that week and the next went very quickly, it was Friday before Esmeralda realized it; the evening before she had filled her room to capacity with all her friends and handed round sherry—good sherry at that, and plates of delicious bits and pieces she had fetched from Fortnum and Mason. There had been a lot of laughter and joking, and although they had talked about her trip to Holland, the reason for her going was passed over lightly, although they had taken it for granted that she would be with them again in two or three months' time.

She hadn't seen much of Leslie, although he had taken her out for a drink earlier in the week and managed to have a quick chat with her when they had met in the hospital. He had adopted a slightly proprietorial role towards her and she rather liked it. No one—no young man, at any rate, had ever been like that before; she blossomed under his attentions, scanty though they were, and when she wished him goodbye she felt emboldened to ask: 'Could you come over and see me? Later, I mean…'

He had responded with flattering eagerness, kissed her lightly and on the plea of urgent work elsewhere, strode away. She had waited to see if he would turn round and wave, but he didn't.

And as for Mr Bamstra, she didn't see him at all; presumably he had gone back to Holland, and in due time she would be put on his theatre list and be just another operation.

She drove herself down to the New Forest in the Mini, crowded round with her possessions, and any half-smothered ideas about Leslie going with her were scotched by his regretful explanation that he had promised to stand in for the Surgical Registrar so that he might go home on family business. She had been disappointed, but there was no point in making a fuss, and he had said that he would come and see her while she was at Leiden—at least, Esmeralda corrected herself, he had almost said so.

She arrived home in a cheerful frame of mind, nonetheless, to be fussed over and spoilt by her mother and Nanny, both of whom talked of nothing else but her forthcoming journey. Leslie wasn't mentioned at all, but Mr Bamstra was, frequently, but in an oblique, vague fashion which made him not so much a person as a nebulous fount of wisdom. The two days passed too quickly, Nanny occupying them in going over Esmeralda's clothes and re-packing them in what she considered to be the correct manner, and Esmeralda and her mother pottering round the garden, which they both loved, or going for gentle walks in the forest while they made plans about telephoning each other and when and where they would do so.

She left on Sunday, driving her mother's Rover, with her parent beside her and Nanny on the back seat. They would see her off and then drive back to Burley, and now that she was on the point of going, Esmeralda had the unpleasant feeling that she was being hustled and bustled into a situation she wasn't too keen about. After all, supposing her foot couldn't be put right, supposing Mr Bamstra made a botch of

it…impossible of course, she couldn't imagine him
making a botch of anything, all the same… She shook
off a vague depression, made cheerful conversation
all the way to the airport and bade her companions
goodbye in a bright voice, even making a little joke
about dancing to meet them the next time she saw
them, and then followed the rest of the passengers to
the aeroplane.

It took her most of the short journey to talk herself
into a rational state of mind, but by the time they
touched down at Schiphol she was, outwardly at least,
quite composed, and allowed herself to be wafted
along the telescopic corridor to the airport itself,
where she transferred herself to the travelator. Once
in the reception area, she found her luggage, offered
her passport for inspection and then made a little hes-
itantly for the Tourist Bureau in the centre of the vast
place; she had been asked to wait there when she had
telephoned the time of her arrival and the unknown,
friendly voice which had answered her had been very
insistent about that.

She stood quietly, a porter beside her, and wondered which of the mass of people milling around her
would be the one looking for her. None of them, as
it turned out; Esmeralda was eyeing a matronly lady
obviously in search of someone and wondering if she
should accost her, when she was tapped on the shoulder, and when she turned round it was to find Mr
Bamstra, elegant and cool in a thin tweed suit, smiling

pleasantly down at her. His hullo was friendly and he
followed it with a conventional 'Welcome to my
country, Esmeralda,' as he turned to speak to the porter. As the three of them set off, Esmeralda said tar-
dily: 'Hullo—I didn't expect to see you.'

'I try to keep Sundays free,' he told her gravely.
'The car's through this door.'

He led the way outside to a crowded car park, and
she wondered, as she limped along beside him, which
of the cars would be his. There was a predominance
of small, ugly Citroëns, large handsome Citroëns, and
Mercedes, but none of these were his. He stopped
beside a Bristol 114, large, elegant, and a pleasing
shade of dark grey; a very expensive car, she knew
that, with a subdued, understated style which made
the cars around it look a little vulgar. She thanked the
porter, got into the front seat at Mr Bamstra's invitation, and waited while the porter was tipped, her
baggage stowed and her companion had taken his
place beside her.

'It was kind of you to meet me,' she observed as
he wove his way towards the motorway running close
to the airport. 'Are we going straight to the hospital?'

He eased the Bristol into the traffic and began to
overtake everything on the road ahead of him, driving
very fast and yet with such an easy manner that he
might have been tooling along a country lane. Esmeralda thought of Leslie and his flamboyant driving
and dismissed the idea as disloyal, then was recalled

to the present by her companion's: 'No, I'm taking
you to spend the night with friends of mine—Adam
and Loveday de Wolff van Ozinga—he and I were
students together and Loveday is English. When I
mentioned that you were coming over to have your
foot put right they insisted that you should go to them
first. They live in Friesland, near Sneek—we'll be
there for supper and I'll pick you up tomorrow morning and take you down to Leiden. I'm doing the foot
on Tuesday.'

She said: 'How kind,' and then: 'But wouldn't it
have been much easier for you if you had taken me
straight to the hospital?'

'Much easier, but not nearly as nice.'

There really wasn't an answer to that one, so she
asked: 'Do you live in Leiden?'

'Er—no, I share my time between Utrecht and
Leiden for the most part—there is a big orthopaedic
clinic just outside Leiden, but I have beds in the general hospital too. My home is nicely in the middle of
these three places—so convenient.'

He allowed the car to skim past a stream of traffic
and she realized that he didn't intend to tell her any
more than that. All right, she thought crossly, if he
wants to be cagey, let him—very mean, really, after
going to her home without a by-your-leave…

Her small, ordinary face assumed an expression of
hauteur which her companion saw; the gleam in his
grey eyes was the only sign of his amusement as he

commented smoothly: 'We're skirting Amsterdam now and pick up the motorway to Alkmaar very shortly—not an exciting road, I'm afraid, but quick. Once we get to Alkmaar, we will cut across the polderland to the Afsluitdijk. We skirt Haarlem too, which is a pity, for there is a great deal to see there, but I promise you that before you go back to England you shall have an opportunity to see some of our cities.'

It seemed only a very short time before he said: 'There's Alkmaar ahead of us; we don't go into the town, but once we turn off the road is rather pretty. Would you like to stop for coffee?'

'Yes, please,' said Esmeralda at once. 'I was excited and not a bit hungry.'

They were already heading away from Alkmaar. 'There's a pleasant place about fifteen minutes ahead.' He slowed the car's pace a little. 'I hope your mother and Nanny Toms are well?'

'Yes, they saw me off—we drove up in Mother's Rover and she was going to drive Nanny back home. They're both quite sure that you're going to cure my foot.'

'And you're not, Esmeralda?'

He had slipped easily enough into calling her by her Christian name, hadn't he? Was that to emphasise the difference in their status? She hardly thought so. Perhaps it was to remind her that he was a good deal older than she was—she had no idea how old; it pleased her to think that she might be able to find out quite a lot about him from these friends they were going to. She said simply: 'Yes, I'm sure too, and anyway, when you want something very much it happens, doesn't it?'

'I agree with you—I believe it's called positive thinking, but I prefer to think of it as pure optimism.'

He had turned into a short side road leading to a long, low, terraced restaurant, and Esmeralda was grateful to him when he parked so close to the entrance that she had only a yard or two to limp, and he made it easier still by strolling along beside her without offering an arm or asking her if she could manage the steps. He chose a table close by and ordered coffee. 'I don't dare to offer you anything else or Loveday will have my head,' he apologised, 'but perhaps I can remedy that later on.'

She imagined him to be making the kind of polite remark one made on such occasions, and said in her turn: 'That would be nice!' Then she asked: 'Where are we now?'

'Very nearly at the Afsluitdijk; that's about twenty miles long and a very fast road, and once in Friesland we should be at the Ozingas' home very quickly, for it's only another twenty miles or so.'

The Bristol tore along, unhindered by traffic; the dyke was straight and they could see ahead of them for miles, half way across Esmeralda exclaimed like an excited child: 'Oh, look—there's the coast of Friesland!' and listened while her companion explained the lie of the land to her, an exercise which lasted until they were on dry land again, and driving down the coast of the Ijsselmeer.

'Bolsward,' said Mr Bamstra briefly as they skirted a small town with a great many picturesque spires and gabled roofs. And a few minutes later: 'Sneek.'

He turned off just outside the town on to a country road running between lakes, and presently reached a small village, and on its further side, the Ozingas' house. It was a large, square red brick building, standing in a quite beautiful garden, but Esmeralda barely had time to glimpse it before they drew up before its solid front door, which was opened with such alacrity that she could only suppose that someone had been on the watch for them. The door-opener was a large man, very much of Mr Bamstra's size but a year or so older. He said: 'Hullo, there,' in a soft, slow voice, gave his friend a friendly thump on the shoulder which would have felled a lesser man, and smiled charmingly at Esmeralda. 'I'm Adam,' he volunteered, 'and you are the Esmeralda Thimo has told us about.' He offered a hand and engulfed hers in it. 'Loveday won't be a moment; she's been hovering for hours and now little Adam, in his ill-timed way, has chosen to sick up. Come in.' He looked across at Mr Bamstra. 'You'll stay for supper? You can't expect Toukje to cook for you at this hour.'

Esmeralda stored the strange sounding name away in the back of her head. Later, given the opportunity,

she would find out about the owner of it. It was a
little disquieting, although she didn't know why, to
hear Mr Bamstra say casually: 'I wouldn't expect her
to, you know. But she would all the same—we have
a wonderful relationship.'

She pondered this remark as they entered the house
and then forgot it at once because there was so much
to see. She hadn't been to Holland before, but she
had seen prints and pictures and read books, so that
the tiled floor, plastered walls and delicately plastered
ceiling weren't a surprise. It was the solid richness of
everything which took her breath; she doubted if anyone in the house knew what the word plastic meant,
although it was obvious to her female eye that the
good old-fashioned elbow grease was not only known
well, but used. She tore her eyes from a delightfully
arranged vase of flowers on the solid hall table and
caught Mr Bamstra's interested gaze. He didn't speak,
however, because someone was coming down the
staircase—Loveday; it couldn't be anyone else, for no
other girl could have been such a splendid foil for
Adam Ozinga's outsize good looks. She was dark and
pretty, and unlike Esmeralda, who couldn't suppress
a twinge of envy at the sight of her, tall and well
built. She raced down the handsome staircase and
went straight to Esmeralda. 'Oh, I'm so glad you've
come,' she cried, 'even if it is only for a few hours—
I wish you could stay longer, but next time you shall.'
She turned to offer a cheek to Mr Bamstra.

'Prettier than ever,' he declared. 'How's my god-son?'

'Almost as big as his father.' She slipped a hand, into her husband's with the unself-consciousness of a child. 'Adam, take Thimo to see him while I take Esmeralda to her room, then we can have supper.'

The room was beautiful. Esmeralda tidied herself while her hostess kept up a flow of small talk, never once giving her an opening to ask a single question about Mr Bamstra, although she did manage to en-quire as they went downstairs: 'Is that Mr Bamstra's name... T something—I've never heard it before.'

'Nice, isn't it? It's Friesian, of course. It sounds like Teemow, doesn't it, but it's spelt Thimo—you can spell it with an E too, which adds to the confu-sion. Some of the Friesian names are very strange, but you won't have to bother with Dutch while you're in Leiden—almost everyone speaks some sort of En-glish.'

They had reached the hall and were making for a half-open arched door behind which they could hear the men laughing and talking. 'Did Thimo tell you that I had been a nurse?'

'No...' Esmeralda would have liked to ask a few leading questions, but once again was frustrated by their arrival in the sitting room—an enormous apart-ment and very beautiful, with its white-painted walls and large, comfortable furniture. She accepted a glass of sherry from her host and sat down beside him, answering his casual, friendly questions happily enough. Her arrival in Holland hadn't been quite what she had expected, but it was nevertheless more than pleasant. After a little while she began to ask a few discreet questions herself, but when she thought them over later on, she was forced to the conclusion that the answers had been vague to the point of nothing at all.

Dinner was fun—the two men were old friends and Loveday was a good hostess. Esmeralda, who had a nice healthy appetite, did full justice to the iced soup, the light-as-air cheese soufflé accompanied by a mouthwatering salad, and finally an ice pudding smothered in whipped cream. They were served by a stoutly built middle-aged woman with a happy face, who, when Loveday said: 'This is our housekeeper and good friend, Saskia,' shook hands with Esmeralda and gave her much the same look that Nanny Toms gave to strangers; kind but slightly reserved, and faintly speculative. Esmeralda, who didn't mind being looked over in the least, smiled back at her and went to sit opposite Mr Bamstra, who leaned across the table to ask if she had seen his godson. The talk went well after that, and she, a little nervous of those who could not only speak another language fluently but crack jokes and be witty in it as well, drew consolation from Loveday's remark that she herself, after more than a year of marriage, was still far from perfect in the Dutch language, and began to enjoy herself.

Mr Bamstra went shortly after they had had their coffee, asking Esmeralda as they said their good nights if she would be ready the following morning directly after breakfast. 'I've an afternoon list,' he explained, 'but I should like to see you settled in first.'

She assured him that she would be ready for him and watched him walk away across the hall beside his friend, feeling lonely at the sight of his broad back disappearing through the door. It must have shown on her face, for Loveday said quickly: 'Shall we go and have a peep at little Adam?' and ushered her up the staircase. Crossing the wide corridor which overlooked the hall, she spoke again. 'Do you mind talking about your op? If you do, just say so, and we won't mention it.'

'I don't mind a bit,' said Esmeralda, 'not with Mr Bamstra or you or your husband, though some people are awful. They pity me, you know, and say awful things like: "And how dreadful for you not being able to dance, dear," or, "Does your poor foot hurt much?"' She turned her green eyes on to her companion. 'I could kill them!'

'Well, you won't get any of that here—sympathy, mostly unsaid, and as much practical help as you want. Thimo's super at his job, but you know that already, don't you? He's hardly a man to boast of his own importance, but it filters through just the same.'

They had paused to stand comfortably side by side, their elbows on the brass rail which topped the balustrade running along one side of the corridor, so that they could look down on to the hall below. Saskia came out of the sitting room just then and saw them, calling something softly to Loveday as she passed beneath them.

'Are you a baroness?' asked Esmeralda, who had sharp ears.

'Well—yes, but only because Adam's a baron. Titles in Holland aren't a bit the same as they are in England, you know—you can't be made a baron or a *jonkheer,* you just are that if your father was, and his father before him, but new ones are never created. It's complicated. The *Adel*—that's the titled families— mostly marry amongst themselves, too.'

'Adam married you,' Esmeralda pointed out.

Loveday turned her lovely face to hers and her smile was a delight. 'Yes, he did, didn't he? And it was the most wonderful thing that ever happened to me.'

She turned away and led the way across the corridor towards a narrow passage leading off it, volunteering as she went: 'Thimo is a *jonkheer,* he's a professor of surgery as well, but he likes to be called mister when he's in England—perhaps you didn't know?'

'No, I didn't.' Esmeralda seized her opportunity. 'Is he...' She got no further, for Loveday had opened a door half way down the passage and beckoned her in. Small Adam at two months of age was easily identifiable as his father's son, for he was the image of his proud parent, and if his size was anything to go by, bid fair to top his father by an inch or so by the time he had finished growing.

His doting mother bent over the cot. 'He's as good as gold,' she said proudly, 'large and placid, just like Adam—as long as he gets his own way if he's made up his mind to something.' She laid gentle fingers on his blond head and they crept out again. 'We've got a Friesian nanny for him, because Adam says he must speak Fries as well as English and Dutch at home. At school he'll be stuffed with Latin and German and French.' She smiled at Esmeralda's look of astonishment. 'They like speaking other people's languages, you know. Shall we go downstairs for half an hour? Adam will be in the sitting room.'

Esmeralda went to bed an hour or so later, and up in her charming room, getting ready for the night, she thought about Mr Bamstra, a little piqued that although he had been friendly enough, he had seemed to hold her at arm's length all the evening. She wished she knew more about him; so far she had learned just about nothing, and there would be little chance to ask questions in the morning. She was still pondering the best way of finding out what she wanted to know when she fell asleep. She hadn't thought once about her operation, nor, for that matter, about Leslie.

In their vast room across the corridor Loveday danced across the thickly carpeted floor to her dressing table. 'Oh, Adam, isn't it wonderful?'

He stood by the door, watching her, smiling. 'I can think of a great many things that are wonderful, my love.'

His wife grinned at him. 'You mean little Adam...'

He nodded. 'But you first, Loveday—you will always be first.'

She had kicked off her shoes, now she flew back on her stockinged feet to fling herself into his arms. 'You say the nicest things,' she told him, and gave him a kiss, 'but what I meant was...'

'I know—isn't it wonderful that the pair of them are in love. You may be right, darling, although I'm sure that Esmeralda has no inkling.'

'But Thimo has.'

He said placidly, his eyes twinkling: 'We had a little talk while you two girls were upstairs.' He put an arm round her shoulders and they crossed the room once more, and she sat down and began to take the pins out of her hair, wisely saying nothing, to be rewarded presently by his: 'What a clever little wife you are, dearest. Tell me, did she ask any questions about Thimo? She had a go at me before dinner—in the nicest possible way, of course.' He added thoughtfully: 'She's curious about him, but at present she's totally unaware.'

'And a lot of good her questions did,' commented Loveday. 'I don't suppose you answered one of them. She asked me one or two, but I didn't tell her anything, more by chance than fortune.'

'Well, don't—Thimo has his plans and he likes to do his own courting.'

'You men and your plans!' said his wife tartly.

'And look where mine led me,' Adam invited her as he bent to kiss her.

Esmeralda, untroubled by the speculations around her, slept like a child and was up, dressed and breakfasted by the time Mr Bamstra arrived. She discovered that she was glad to see him again, even though she was bursting with curiosity about him and there had been no chance to discover the simplest facts about him—where he lived, how old he was, if he were married. She paid a lightning visit to the nursery, bade her new friends a warm goodbye and found herself in the car once more, being driven away amidst a rain of 'Come agains' and 'See you soons.'

She sat silent because Mr Bamstra, beyond his brief greeting, had made no effort at conversation, and she wondered why it was that she had such a strong urge to find out all about him when they were practically strangers; indeed the urge was strong enough for her to consider asking a question or two. She was trying to decide between 'I hope you found your wife well' and 'I expect your wife misses you when you're away', both leading questions which he would surely have to answer however much he disliked doing so, when he spoke first.

'I'm taking you straight to the hospital. You will be in the Private Wing—the Sister there and several of the nurses speak English. My registrar Octavius Barmond, is young, clever and should prove helpful to you.'

'Oh—won't you be there?' Esmeralda's voice sounded forlorn and she looked at her companion anxiously; she could only see his profile, but it looked as calm and good-natured as usual and she couldn't see the gleam in his eyes.

'Er—yes, but not of course each and every day; I have to go to Utrecht this week and I must return to Groningen at the weekend.'

She stared at a windmill they were passing. So he had a wife. 'But you'll do the operation?'

'Of course. I think you'll find the Ward Sister a very nice girl; she will see that you get the English papers and tea with milk and all that sort of thing.'

'That will be very nice,' she declared, 'and thank you for thinking of it.' She added defiantly: 'I'm not a bit nervous.'

He glanced at her quickly and away again. 'Excited rather, I imagine—very soon now you will be able to start planning your future.'

Which reminded her of Leslie. She felt ashamed

that she had forgotten him—no, not forgotten; there had been so much to think about. She agreed in a subdued voice and asked where they were.

'Lemmer.' He sounded relieved to be changing the conversation. 'We're back down the opposite side of the Ijsselmeer; presently we cross reclaimed land, then through Kampen and on to the motorway to Zwolle. We stay on it until we reach Hilversum; Leiden is another forty miles from there. We'll stop for coffee, I think.'

They stopped in pleasant wooded country somewhere on the road between Zwolle and Hilversum and had their coffee on the terrace of an attractive café, and her companion made delightful small talk about nothing at all, and when they were back in the car once more, he took upon himself the task of pointing out the more interesting aspects of the countryside through which they were driving. It seemed no time at all before Esmeralda exclaimed: 'That must be Leiden over there,' and it was. He slowed the car to go into the city, turning and twisting through narrow streets and stopping at last in the hospital's rather splendid courtyard.

He got out and opened the door and took her hand. 'Leave the luggage,' he told her, 'and come with me.' He smiled as he spoke and her sudden unpleasant sensation of fright disappeared. She said: 'Of course, Mr Bamstra,' in her usual sensible voice and limped

briskly beside him and up the steps and in through
the massive glass swing doors, still with her hand
in his.

CHAPTER FOUR

ESMERALDA heard Mr Bamstra's voice long before she could see him; it was at the other end of a quite pleasant tunnel of grey cloud, through which she was drifting. She became aware that it was his hand which held hers, too, and when he said: 'Wake up now, Esmeralda,' in a quiet, commanding voice, she squeezed the hand to let him know that although she had heard him she wasn't going to be bothered. It was his low laugh which made her change her wandering mind. She pushed away the last comforting shreds of cloud and opened her eyes.

He filled the whole of her view, enormous in his theatre gown, his cap and mask hiding all but the high bridge of his nose and his eyes. She said hullo in a woolly voice, and then: 'You do look enormous,' and struggled to focus him clearly as she went on politely: 'You don't mind if I go back to sleep again?' and did so.

When she opened her eyes again, he was there— much clearer this time, still in his theatre clothes, but now his mask was pulled down under his chin. When he didn't speak she swallowed from a dry mouth and said with faint peevishness: 'I said I wanted to go to sleep.'

She watched his faint smile come and go. 'So you did—four hours ago. I've been back to theatre and finished my afternoon list while you snored.'

Her eyes flew wide at that. 'Snored—Oh, I don't. It's all done, isn't it?' She looked the question she couldn't put into words.

'And very successfully, though I've never seen such a minced-up set of metatarsals in my life. Would you like a cup of tea?'

She smiled slowly, relief and happiness washing over her so that she found it difficult to speak. 'More than anything else in the world,' she told him, and turned her head to look around her. She was back in the little room they had taken her to on the previous day, in her own nightie again, the offending limb concealed under a cradle. 'When may I get up?' she wanted to know, not really caring if he answered or not, for she felt sleepy again.

Perhaps that was why he didn't answer; her lids drooped and she heard him say: 'I'll be back,' and when she dragged them apart again, he had gone, and a nurse was standing by her bed with a tray set with its little teapot and milk jug and cup and saucer; it reminded Esmeralda so forcibly of home that quite unusual tears filled her eyes and tumbled down her pale cheeks. The nurse put down her tray, making soothing sounds in her own language, and swept an arm round her shoulders. 'First the cry, then the tea,' she said comfortably, and sent a reassuring smile over her shoulder to Mr Bamstra, standing in the doorway.

Esmeralda felt better when she had had her little weep. She drank her tea, apologised to the nurse for making a fool of herself, and went to sleep again. The pain in her foot woke her this time; a dull ache which curled itself round her bones and up her leg, and when she tried to shift her foot to ease the pain a little, the heavy plaster prevented her. There was a bell on the bedside table, but having answered so many bells herself, she was hesitant to give someone else that trouble. She saw with surprise that it was evening; she must have slept on and off all day, and now to add to her distress, she discovered that she was dreadfully thirsty too, although the pain was swamping everything now. She made herself lie still, knowing that someone would be round on a routine visit before long and she could hold out until then. But the pain became steadily worse, she could feel sweat trickling down her forehead—it was no good, she would have to ring.

But there was no need after all. 'Pain bad?' asked Mr Bamstra from the door, and was by her bed before he had finished speaking, taking her pulse. 'Why didn't you ring sooner?'

'I've only been awake a few minutes,' she managed with a smile, 'and I knew a nurse would be along.' She hardly noticed when he wiped her forehead; she certainly didn't see him press the bell.

A nurse came at once and he said something quietly to her and she disappeared again. 'You must be feeling hungry,' he said in a placid voice. 'You're going to have something to check the pain and then you will feel like eating—and what about one of your nice cups of tea?'

'Lovely,' she spoke through gritted teeth, 'but please don't let them bother about anything for me to eat.' She glanced out of the window. 'It must be quite late in the evening.' She looked at him, trying to smile; he was in an elegant grey suit, which must surely mean that his day's work was done—the night staff would be on duty shortly and they would have enough to do without feeding her…

'Now that is a pity, for I thought that I might have some coffee while you ate your supper. I got away later than usual and I don't expect to get my supper until the very end of the evening.'

The nurse had come back, produced her syringe and given its contents as he spoke, and Esmeralda, whose hands had been tightly clasped, slowly uncurled them and relaxed a little.

'Give it a couple of minutes,' encouraged Mr Bamstra, and turned away to say something to the nurse, who went away again with a smiling nod as he crossed the room to sit in the small wooden chair provided for visitors, but it creaked so alarmingly under his weight that he got up again and came to sit very carefully on the side of the bed. He didn't speak or move for a few minutes; only when she said on a relieved sigh; 'Oh, that's better,' did he look at her. 'Good, and now listen to me. When the pain returns, which I am afraid it will do for the first couple of days, you are to say so without delay—it doesn't help your recovery if you are in pain, you know.' He smiled. 'Do you like talking? I'll not apologise for discussing your foot over supper; nurses, I believe, have a habit of talking shop at their meals.'

'So do doctors!'

His eyes twinkled. 'How right you are! Has the pain gone completely?'

She nodded. 'I feel marvellous now, thank you. I hope I haven't been a nuisance to everyone.'

'Not in the least. Want to see the foot?'

'Please.'

He got up and took the sheet off the cradle, revealing her smoothly plastered foot and leg. The cast had been cut away in front so that the actual site of the operation could be inspected and got at if necessary. There were little steel pins sticking out of the tops of her toes; she inspected them without comment and asked: 'No weights?'

'No—all the bones are back where they should be. I had to shape them up a bit; there were quite a few spurs and I chiselled off the odd bits and realigned them.' He looked at her squarely. 'Both your feet are exactly alike now, Esmeralda.'

'I'll never be able to thank you enough. It's like a

miracle, it is a miracle really, and you did it. It must
have taken a long time.'

'So-so.' He pulled up the light easy chair ready for
her use when she was allowed out of bed, and sat
down cautiously. 'That's better—were you quite comfortable yesterday?'

Yesterday seemed a long way off when she thought
about it. He had brought her up to the fourth floor
where the Private Wing was and introduced her to the
Ward Sister, accepted a cup of coffee, and sat down
to chat about nothing much for ten minutes—that had
been kind of him, for she had had the time to get used
to the strangeness of it all before he declared that he
had better be off to theatre to see Sister about some
changes he wanted made in the afternoon's list. He
had barely gone before Esmeralda was swept along
to her room, shown where everything was, told at
what times her meals would be served and had the
telephone explained to her.

'Very comfortable,' she said. 'What nice girls the
nurses are—and Sister. I had no idea that it would be
as pleasant as this—and a room to myself, too. Do
all your National Health patients have rooms like this
one?'

'When it is considered desirable,' he said quietly.
'I fancy I can hear your supper coming.'

It was rusks and yoghurt and the promised tea, and
because she felt so much better she viewed with envy
the large pile of sandwiches which had accompanied

Mr Bamstra's coffee. He caught the look and chuckled. 'Still hungry?' he asked, and crossed to the bed to hand her a cheese sandwich. 'But that's the only one, mind, and for heaven's sake don't tell anyone, or I shall get shot.'

He watched her gobble it down and then pour the last of the tea. 'Would you like to telephone your mother?'

'Oh, may I? I told her not to worry about today, that I'd call her in the morning.'

'I let her know that everything was successful as soon as you were out of theatre, but she'll want to hear your voice.'

Esmeralda nodded and asked rather shyly: 'Mr Bamstra, have you a mother?'

For a moment he looked utterly astonished, then he answered gravely: 'Certainly, and sisters.'

'That's why you understand.'

He said nothing to this but went to plug in the telephone and get the number for her. He had come to sit on the edge of the bed once more the better to do it, which gave her a splendid opportunity to study his face at close quarters. It was a very handsome face, though not so young, and his hair, now that she could have a good look, was almost as silver as it was fair.

He spoke to the operator and then said quietly: 'I'm thirty-eight and I have a great many grey hairs.'

Esmeralda gave a gasp. 'I do beg your pardon...I

was only wondering...I didn't know you were looking—you didn't seem to be.'

He gave her a quick amused glance. 'And you're
twenty-six and there isn't a grey hair in that nice
mousey head of hair, is there?' He spoke into the
telephone and then handed the receiver to her. 'Here
is your call.'

Her mother's voice was very clear in her ear. 'Darling? How lovely to hear you, and what wonderful
news! Thimo told me and I can hardly believe it. How
do you feel?'

'Marvellous,' Esmeralda assured her, not quite
truthfully. 'I can't believe it's all over.'

'You're tired; I can hear it in your voice, but just
to hear you...here's Nanny.'

Nanny's voice, sharp and firm, came over the line.
'I can't think of anything to say, Miss Esmeralda, I
can't abide these telephones—you know how happy
I am for you, bless you. Is that good man with you?'

'Yes, Nanny, he is.'

'I knew it,' said Nanny in a satisfied voice. 'Now
you just go to sleep like a good girl, and that'll please
your old Nanny more than anything else.'

'Yes, Nanny, I will—good night,' and a moment
later: 'Good night, Mother dear.'

Mr Bamstra took the receiver from her and she
yawned widely, caught his eye and gave a small,
weary laugh. 'Oh, dear, I don't suppose a girl has ever
yawned in your face before!' She was half asleep

again. 'It's not because I don't like you,' she assured him, mumbling a little as her eyelids drooped. 'Isn't it funny to think that when I was born you were eleven years old?'

She didn't wait for an answer to this remark but tucked her cheek into the pillow and slept, her mouth a little open so that now and then she gave a delicate small snore. Mr Bamstra got up from the bed and stood looking at her; he looked for quite some time before he went to find the night nurse so that he might give his instructions for the night.

Esmeralda woke very early the next morning. The sky was already bright and she could hear the sparrows twittering on the ledges and gables of the hospital. Far away there were the first faint sounds of traffic, and presently the city's clocks struck the hour and played a little tune as well. She lay and listened to them, aware of what had awakened her; the pain in her foot, rapidly mounting from a dull ache to a fierce red-hot agony. She bore it for a short time, but it didn't lessen, so she rang the bell, feeling mean because she was bothering the nurses who would have enough to do at that hour, and almost at once a nurse came in with a cheerful, 'Good morning, Miss Jones.' She lifted her hand to show the syringe in its little dish. 'You see that we are ready and waiting, for Professor Bamstra says, "An injection is to be given on the instant that Miss Jones wakes, for there is much pain"!' She slid the needle into Esmeralda's arm as she spoke and then gave her a motherly pat. 'Very soon the pain is gone and then I will bring the tea.'

Esmeralda's pinched face broke into a smile. 'You are a dear—thank you very much. Would you call me Esmeralda?'

'That is your name? Mine is Anna, I am here at night, and at eight o'clock Syja will come—you met her yesterday. And now the tea.'

Esmeralda was pouring her second cup when Mr Bamstra walked in. He said 'Hullo,' and then: 'Still drinking tea? Is the pain easing?'

She was aware of a deep pleasure at the sight of him, quite forgetting what a sight she must look with her shiny, pallid face and damp, untidy hair no longer neatly plaited. She said quickly: 'I'm fine, thank you—you've been up, haven't you? Would you like some tea? There's a glass...'

He looked tired and his chin was bristly and he was wearing the slacks and sweater that most medical men wore when they were called out at night.

But he wasn't so tired that he couldn't examine her foot properly. 'Very nice,' he pronounced. 'You'll be up in a chair this morning.' He smiled at her. 'Yes, we've been up—quite a few of us, I'm afraid—a nasty multiple crash. Nice of you to offer your tea, but Anna is making me some coffee before I go. Octavius will be along to see you after breakfast.'

He had gone with a casual nod, leaving her feeling flat, but really there had been nothing for him to stay for, she told herself, looking dispassionately at her face in the hand mirror; she had never had illusions about her commonplace features, and a good thing too, for never had she appeared so plain and unattractive.

She felt better about it when she had breakfasted, bathed and been helped into a chair by the open window. It had been too much effort to put her hair up, but she had brushed it and tied it back with a ribbon and taken the greatest of pains with her face, so that, decked out in the pink nightie and gown her mother had given her, she wasn't ill pleased with her appearance.

'And now let Mr Bamstra come,' she told herself; he would find a quite different girl from the frowsty creature he had talked to at five o'clock that morning. Only he didn't come, only his registrar, Octavius, who examined her swollen, discoloured foot with its hideous little pins, made sure that the plaster wasn't too tight, enquired as to health and studied her charts, all without once mentioning his chief. He didn't seem in much of a hurry either, and when Zuster van Nelle came quietly in to join them, his pace became even slower. Esmeralda, her romantic nose a-twitch, sensed something in the air and had this confirmed by the glances the two of them exchanged, and which she watched with all the sympathy of someone who was in love too. She liked Octavius, although he was a little serious-minded for her taste, and Monique van

Nelle was just right for him; quiet and unflappable, with a pretty fairness and mild blue eyes—she was a first-rate nurse, too. Happily matchmaking, she suggested that they might have their coffee together. 'Would it matter awfully?' she asked, 'just for this morning—and would you call me Esmeralda?'

The other girl smiled. 'Of course, and we will have coffee here too. Usually we have it in the office, but if you don't mind that we speak our own language when we discuss the patients, then it does not matter.'

Esmeralda agreed happily and they had their elevenses together, and after a few minutes of casual talk they did what she had hoped they would do, lapsed into their own tongue, and she felt pretty sure that a great part of their conversation at least wasn't about the patients at all. She sat back, feeling pleased with herself, contemplating her foot and hoping that they were making a date.

Mr Bamstra didn't come all day. Esmeralda read, did some knitting in a peevish way, slept a little and wrote letters to her mother, her friends at Trent's and a short, non-committal one to Leslie. She had expected him to telephone and he hadn't, and although she wouldn't admit it to herself, she had half hoped that he would send her some flowers—after all, it was an easy matter these days and not beyond his pocket. She had had a great bunch of summer flowers from the girls at Trent's, as well as roses from her mother and Nanny, and a great many cards besides. Perhaps, she told herself, making excuses for him, he had been too busy; it was hard to find time for such things when one's day was filled from end to end.

The unwilling thought that Mr Bamstra's day had been filled from end to end and had even oveflowed into the night hours, and yet he had found time to come and see her, didn't help in the least, even though she told herself sharply that it was his job to come anyway—she was his patient—but surely not at five o'clock in the morning after spending half the night in theatre? She decided not to think about it any more, for it was giving her a headache, and although they had been careful to keep her free from pain all day, she felt tired and irritable. She flung down the knitting she had been pretending to do and picked up a book and read the same page over and over again without seeing a word of it until Syja brought her supper tray.

She ate it obediently, anxious not to be a nuisance to anyone, and allowed herself to be put to bed with the minimum of trouble. Tomorrow would be another day; there would be letters or a telephone call, and she would try out her crutches for the first time. She was to use them only for a few days, for once Mr Bamstra was satisfied that the foot was healing cleanly, the heel of her plaster would be strengthened and she would be allowed to get around with a stout stick. Monique and Syja came to say goodnight presently, and then Anna popped in to pass the time of day when she had taken the report. Esmeralda assured them all that she was free from pain, very sleepy and wanted for nothing, and resolutely closed her eyes.

She kept them shut for almost two hours, pretending that the faint nagging pain in her foot would go away at any minute now, not admitting to herself that even worse than the pain was the doubt that Leslie hadn't meant what he said.

'You are to have this,' said Anna softly in her ear. 'You have pain, yes, although you lie there with your eyes shut. Professor Bamstra says that you must sleep, so you will drink this, please. Tomorrow the pain will be better.'

And Esmeralda, weary of her thoughts, drank down whatever it was and was thankful to feel the pain receding, and very soon a delightful sleepiness took possession of her. Her head drooped on the pillows, and she slept—so soundly that when Mr Bamstra came in at one o'clock in the morning, she didn't stir.

She made splendid progress. She mastered the crutches in no time at all, and went up and down the wide corridor of the wing, a little apprehensive about falling over or catching her wretched little wires on something, but she mastered this weakness too and stomped around, careful not to get in the busy nurses' way. She still had pain, but it was less now and was to be expected; a great deal of calcification had had to be broken down and there had been a good deal of chipping and hammering. She did her best to bear it for as long as possible and on the whole, managed very well.

It was towards the second day of using her crutches that she was promenading up and down the corridor, her mind busy with the problem of Leslie; there was still no letter, no card even, from him. The temptation to telephone him was very great, but she had little experience of such a situation and was uncertain what to do. She swung along, her head down, her hair hanging round her shoulders in an untidy tangle. She stopped and tossed it impatiently down her back, feeling hot and tired and aimless, so that when she caught sight of Mr Bamstra standing at the far end of the corridor, watching her, she cried quite crossly: 'Where have you been? It's three days!'

If he found this greeting surprising, he gave no sign of it. His 'Hullo, Esmeralda,' was quietly friendly, but somehow it reminded her who he was so that she paused to look at him and then hobbled as fast as she could towards him. 'I'm sorry, I don't know why I said that—you've been busy...'

'And so have you, I see.' He gave her an encouraging smile. 'We'll have that heel strengthened today, and then you can get around even faster. How does it feel?'

It was funny how he always made her feel better. 'Marvellous. It aches a bit—it will be nice to get rid of these pins, though.'

'A week or two yet, I'm afraid. Will you come into

your room and I'll take a look.' He raised his voice in a mild bellow for Monique van Nelle and when she came, placid and smiling as she always was, ushered the two of them into Esmeralda's room, where he spent a considerable time gently prodding with his large sensitive fingers, and finally stood back satisfied.

'Very nice. Monique, we'll have that heel seen to—let me see, what have we got this afternoon? Shall we say six o'clock this evening in the plaster room? That will give it sufficient time to dry out before Esmeralda gets out of her bed tomorrow morning—and not without your stick, mind. Antibiotics finished? Physio coming each day?'

He nodded to himself and glanced at the Dutch girl. 'Monique, will you get hold of Octavius and let him know, otherwise he might have plans of his own.' His grey eyes twinkled as she went faintly pink. 'Tell him there will be half an hour's work, no more.' And then, when she had gone: 'And now, Esmeralda, tell me why you look like that.'

'Like what?' She was very conscious of her untidy hair; probably her nose was shining too.

'Sad—worried, waiting for something.' He turned his back and went to look out of the window. 'You hear from your mother regularly?'

'Oh, yes—we telephone each other and write letters.' She added with false cheerfulness: 'I get lots of letters.'

'But none from young Chapman.'

She was instantly on the defensive. 'He's busy…' She stopped herself from saying more; the man before her was busy too—busier. 'Perhaps they've got lost in the post,' she mumbled miserably.

He helped her out kindly. 'Oh, probably—in any case, it is very difficult to find time to write, even to telephone after a hard day's work. I think you should allow him a few more days; I daresay it seems a long time to you since you left England, but it's not yet a week, you know.'

He turned round to face her and now his voice was brisk. 'Tomorrow you are to start walking, Esmeralda—with a stick, of course; it may hurt at first, but no harm can come to your foot; it's secure enough in its plaster. We'll have the stitches out in a few days and then it will be just a question of physio and patience. I can promise you that your foot is as near its original form as it's possible to get it.'

She twisted a length of hair and tossed it over her shoulder. 'I'll never be able to thank you enough,' she said soberly. 'You can't imagine what it means to me…' She smiled suddenly: 'I'll be able to dance!'

'Indeed, yes.' He glanced at his watch. 'I must go.'

'Yes, of course. I'm sorry I was cross.' She didn't look at him. 'Have you been to your home since I saw you last?'

She saw the surprise on his face and coloured faintly, although he answered readily enough. 'For a flying visit—Why?' He was interrupted by Monique, who poked her pretty head round the door and said something urgently in her soft voice.

He went to the door, pausing only long enough to say: 'I have to talk to someone on the telephone—*tot ziens.*' The door closed soundlessly behind him.

Esmeralda, left alone, heaved a great sigh of relief. What on earth had possessed her to ask him such a question? It was no business of hers what he did or where he went; he had never volunteered any information about himself, and he must have been wondering what to say to her—what luck that Monique should have come in just then. She went over to the small dressing table and sat down before it to tidy her hair; such a pity that she always looked such a fright when Mr Bamstra came to see her.

The Theatre Block was on the floor beneath the Private Wing, which meant that Esmeralda had to suffer the indignity of a wheelchair to get there. Monique went with her, chatting about nothing much in her adequate English and getting the porter to stop so that Esmeralda could admire the view from the enormous windows in the lift foyer. They were laughing and giggling together over Esmeralda's efforts to speak Dutch as they went towards the theatre unit and when they finally stopped in the plaster room Octavius, waiting for them, observed: 'We could hear you from a great distance; you sounded like a school outing.'

He smiled as he spoke and stared hard at Monique, who pretended not to see him, looking at her, but there was no time to say more, because Mr Bamstra came in, a plastic apron covering most of his vast person, said hullo in a businesslike manner, whisked Esmeralda out of the chair and on to the table, and signified his intention to start work.

The whole business took a good deal less than the half an hour he had promised. Esmeralda, back in her room, leg elevated and drying, felt vaguely let down; she had actually put her hair up and done her face once more, as well as putting on a particularly attractive white peignoir, lavishly trimmed with lace and ribbons. She hadn't been sure why she had gone to so much trouble; perhaps a subconscious wish that Leslie might appear without warning. In any case, it had been a sheer waste of time, for of course there was no sign of Leslie, and as for Mr Bamstra, she reflected sourly, he hadn't looked at her for more than a split second. Upon further reflection, she wondered why that should matter to her.

She was a little excited in the morning. She was a stage nearer being able to walk like everyone else and she put the unwieldy limb to the ground with a feeling of triumph; it felt strange and she would have to get used to balancing on the heel, but it didn't hurt, even though it still looked hideous. By the time Anna came in with her morning tea, she had overcome the strangeness, and even managed, helped by that obliging damsel, to achieve a shower.

It was going to be a hot day again. She plaited her

hair and tied it back neatly, put on one of her pretty gowns and went to sit by the window for her breakfast. She had almost finished it when Monique came in with the post; there were quite a few letters, and at the bottom of the little pile, a telegram. She opened it quickly—it was from Leslie and said simply: 'Delighted to hear everything OK' and was signed simply Leslie. Hardly the same as a letter, even a Get Well card, but at least he had sent something.

Esmeralda frowned; how did he know that everything was OK? She hadn't told him…the frown cleared and she smiled widely; he would have telephoned her mother, of course—probably he had been telephoning each day and her mother had forgotten to tell her. The thought of him going to so much trouble quite obliterated the disappointment at the businesslike wording of the telegram. She read it again, sighed a little and opened the first of her letters.

She had visitors too. She was leaning over the tiny balcony outside her window, when the door opened and Loveday came in with Adam on her heels. 'We would have come before,' she explained, 'but Thimo said we weren't to; you had to concentrate on getting on to your feet without outside distraction.' She kissed Esmeralda's cheek and laid a glorious bunch of flowers on the bed. 'Adam's got a job to do here, so I came with him. He won't be ready until four o'clock, so do you suppose you can put up with me until then?'

Esmeralda said yes with a fervency which made her visitors look at her intently, but they said nothing, and when Monique came in presently, they all had their coffee together, crowded together in the little room, and presently Adam smiled amiably at Esmeralda, kissed his wife and sauntered away towards the Theatre Block, and minutes later Monique went away too, leaving the two girls alone.

'You look marvellous,' said Loveday with more kindness than truth. 'Of course the foot looks like something out of a horror film, doesn't it? But I hear that Thimo has got it just about perfect—it took him three hours.'

'I didn't know. He—he doesn't tell me much and I can't ask questions all the time. There are several things…'

Loveday interrupted her ruthlessly: 'He's in the theatre now—there's a particularly tricky case…' She went on to describe it in some detail and at great length, and led the talk firmly away from Thimo, and indeed, contrived not to mention him for the remainder of her visit, which rather frustrated Esmeralda's curiosity.

But she enjoyed Loveday's company. They got on well, the two of them, and Loveday knew exactly what was expected of her. A few minutes before the patients' midday meal was to be served she declared that she had to see someone living close to the hospital and would be back in an hour or so, so that

Esmeralda ate undistracted by talk and had time for a rest before Loveday returned, bearing an armful of magazines and a basket of fruit. And later, when Adam joined them, he produced a selection of paperbacks and a jigsaw puzzle. 'Can't have you getting bored,' he pronounced as he poured himself a cup of cooling tea. 'Of course you'll come to us when Thimo lets you out.'

Esmeralda's eyes shone greenly. 'Oh, how wonderful—but really I can't put you to all that trouble. I should go home...'

'Of course you should,' agreed Loveday, 'but Thimo won't hear of that for a little while after you leave here; he'll want to keep tabs on you to make sure that everything's going as it should.'

'Oh—well, I should love to come and stay with you for a few days—but it seems a bit much. I mean, I hardly know you...'

'Any friend of Thimo's,' said Adam, 'is a friend of ours.' He gave her a sudden, dazzling smile. 'We'll be in again,' he promised, and looked at his wife. 'Ready, darling?'

It seemed quiet after they had gone. Esmeralda turned on her radio, wrote a letter or two and got out her despised knitting. It had been a very nice day, she reflected; she had had news from Leslie at last, visitors, flowers, books, magazines...there was no reason why she should feel so depressed. She knitted ten rows, hating every one of them, and then bundled her handiwork away and picked up a magazine. If she read it from cover to cover it would take her till supper time, and after that she could go to bed.

She did just that, unconscious of the fact that her ear was cocked for the sound of Mr Bamstra's large feet. An ear cocked in vain.

CHAPTER FIVE

Mr Bamstra came the next morning, a few minutes
after Esmeralda's breakfast tray had been brought in.
He carried a steaming cup of coffee in his hand, and
hard on his heels came Anna, on the point of going
off duty, bearing a plate of buttered toast. His good
morning was genial. 'I have rather a long day before
me,' he explained, his deep voice unhurried, 'and I
left home without my breakfast. I don't like Toujke
to get up at an unreasonable hour, and Anna is always
very kind...'

He sat down on the edge of the bed and put his
toast on her tray. 'You look happier than the last time
I saw you.'

He quite obviously expected an answer, which was
a pity, for she was curious about Toujke and it would
have been an excellent opportunity to have kept her
in the conversation. 'Well, I heard from Leslie.'

He selected a piece of toast with care, not looking
at her. 'And?'

'It was a telegram.'

'How nice—happy now?'

Esmeralda poured more tea. 'Yes, thank you—did
you think me very silly?'

He shook his head. 'Heavens, no. I daresay you'll have a long letter by the next post with some quite ordinary explanation as to why he couldn't write sooner.'

She nodded rather uncertainly, thinking how placid and safe he looked sitting there, munching his toast—someone one could talk to…

'You see, if I were a pretty girl with ordinary feet, I don't suppose I would be so uncertain, would I?' She looked at him anxiously and he smiled encouragingly.

'Now you won't need to feel uncertain any more,' he assured her. 'That foot will be as good as the other one, and it doesn't matter that you're not pretty; you have lovely eyes and a delightful voice. I don't see that you have anything to worry about.'

Perhaps it wasn't a very flattering speech, but he hadn't pretended that she was pretty, which made the rest of what he had said ring true. She smiled a little shyly and thanked him. 'Loveday and Adam came to see me,' she volunteered.

'I know—Adam comes here fairly often, he's by way of being a very good surgeon. He told me that they were going to ask you to stay with them once you are able to leave here.'

'It's very kind of them and I'd love to, only I feel it's an imposition.'

Mr Bamstra had gone to the basin to wash his hands. 'My dear girl, Adam has never been imposed

upon in his life; he arranges everything just as he
wishes it to be and he never allows anything to get
in his way.'

She watched him dry his hands on her towel. 'Are
you like that, too?' she wanted to know.

He screwed the towel into a ball and tossed it on
to the basin. 'Yes, I am.' He spoke seriously and just
for a moment Esmeralda glimpsed someone other
than the elegant man with his placid face and bland
voice; someone who could be ruthless if he wished.
But even as she thought that he had become his normal self once more. She listened to him telling her in
an impersonal voice to use her foot as much as she
could. 'And if it aches at all,' he told her 'Zuster van
Nelle has something for the pain, so don't hesitate to
ask for it.' He was already at the door, his '*tot ziens*'
was brisk as he disappeared.

The day passed quietly. Octavius came and went,
Syja brought her her meals and accompanied her to
physio too, because there was a staircase which Mr
Bamstra said she was to use instead of the lift.
Esmeralda found it a little difficult, but she was beginning to think of her foot as a foot again, even
though it lay so securely in its plaster. She was tired
when she got back to her room, but she didn't mind
that. She didn't mind the lack of post, either, or the
fact that she would have to unpick several rows of
wrongly done knitting; she felt that at last she was
making progress. She felt proud of her efforts on the

stairs; and over and above that, although had nothing to do with it at all, was the pleasant memory of Mr Bamstra's remark about her lovely eyes.

Quite buoyed up, Esmeralda re-did her hair; polished her pretty pink nails and changed into the pink gown. It was a bit silly, really, for it was almost tea time and there would certainly be no visitors.

But there were. She had just arranged the last mousey tress to her satisfaction when Monique put her head round the door, said: 'People to see you Esmeralda,' and withdrew it again to allow Mrs Jones, followed by Nanny, to come in.

'Mother!' shrieked Esmeralda, and stumped across the room to fling herself into her parent's arms. 'And Nanny!' She hugged her too. 'What a simply gorgeous surprise—how did you get here and where are you staying, and why...?'

Her mother sat down and loosened the jacket of her elegant two-piece.

'Well, darling, Nanny and I have talked about you a great deal, and I know we've written to each other and telephoned and Thimo has let me know how you were getting on, but we did want to see you, and yesterday he suggested that we should come over.' She beamed at her daughter. 'So here we are!'

Esmeralda pushed Nanny gently into a chair and went to sit on the bed. 'He never said a word. Did you fly?'

'Yes, and someone met us at the airport and

brought us here, and Thimo will fetch us presently
and drive us to his home. He wasn't quite sure when
he'd be coming, but that nice Sister didn't seem to
think it mattered how long we stayed.'

'You're staying with Mr Bamstra?' Esmeralda was
astounded.

'Yes, dear—just for a couple of nights.'

'Well…how kind of him. I don't even know where
he lives.'

'We don't either,' said her mother cheerfully. 'Now
we want to hear about everything—I know you've
told us all about it on the telephone, but it's never the
same. Let me see your foot.'

Esmeralda lifted the ungainly limb and had it inspected. Her mother uttered a gasp of horror at the
sight of the pins, but Nanny, made of sterner stuff,
had a good look. 'Stands to reason,' she declared sensibly, 'if all those little bones had to be changed, they
would need to be held tight. They look nasty things,
but I daresay they don't hurt once they're in.'

'No, they don't, Nanny,' Esmeralda agreed, 'and
my foot's beginning to look quite a nice colour again.
I walk everywhere on it, too—even stairs.'

'It's quite safe?' her mother wanted to know.
'Won't you damage it when you walk on it?'

'No, darling—it can't move at all, you see, and I
use the rest of my leg, and that's good for the mus-
cles.'

'You're sure it doesn't hurt?'

'Positive, Mother dear—here's tea, good.'

Syja had come in, the ward maid behind her, laden with a tray of tea things, plates of little sandwiches and biscuits. 'The English four o'clock tea,' she announced happily, and stayed to laugh and talk for a minute before leaving them to their refreshment.

'Tea,' said Mrs Jones on a great sigh. 'I'm dying for a cup, and so is Nanny. Our one fear was that we wouldn't be able to get our tea.'

They were nicely embarked on their first cups when the door opened again and Mr Bamstra came in. 'I heard the teacups rattling,' he explained, greeting them. 'Indeed, each time I come—or almost each time—I find Esmeralda with her nose buried in the teapot.'

He sat himself down on the side of the bed and Monique came in with another cup and saucer and said something to him, low-voiced. He looked at his watch and answered her briefly before asking Mrs Jones: 'Will it be all right for you and Miss Toms if I pick you up about six o'clock? I have a case to see in ten minutes, but it won't be going to theatre tonight.' He turned his attention at last to Esmeralda. 'How's the foot? Did you manage the stairs?'

'Quite well, not perhaps as gracefully as I would have liked!'

They all laughed and during the next few minutes she had the opportunity of watching him charm Nanny as well as her mother. Indeed, Nanny unbent so far as to tell him that she had brought him a bottle of her cowslip wine, exclusively for his own use. 'And I would take it as a kindness on your part, sir,' she abjured him, 'if you would call me Nanny.'

And when he thanked her, she nodded her severely coiffed head in its sensible hat and asked: 'And do you have brothers and sisters, Mr Bamstra?'

It disappointed Esmeralda very much when he told her nothing more than: 'Two sisters—married and with children,' before he turned the conversation adroitly. 'Have you always been with Mrs Jones, Nanny?'

The telling of Nanny's busy if uneventful life took up all of the ten minutes he had allowed himself. He got up to go presently, promising to be back as soon as he was able.

He was as good as his word. It still wanted fifteen minutes to the hour when he returned, and within very few minutes ushered Mrs Jones and Nanny out of the room, staying only just long enough to pass the time of day with Esmeralda and assure her that her visitors would be back in the morning. 'You could take them round part of the hospital,' he suggested. 'There's a splendid view from the lift foyer windows.'

'Shall we see you?' asked Mrs Jones as she prepared to accompany him.

'Not very likely, I'm afraid—I have to go to Amsterdam tomorrow, although I shall come here to pick you up about teatime, if that suits you.' He waited patiently while first Mrs Jones and then Nanny embraced Esmeralda, added his own rather casual good night, and escorted them from the room, leaving her feeling forlorn in a room suddenly very empty; he was back again within seconds, however. 'Far be it from me to ignore the bedtime ritual,' he observed blandly, and kissed her too.

By the time Esmeralda saw him late the following afternoon, she had persuaded herself that his gesture had been purely avuncular—offered, as it were, as a mark of his appreciation of her efforts to make a quick recovery. And his manner, when he did come, bore this out. He was charming, as he almost always was, friendly, and just a little withdrawn—certainly he showed no sign of awareness of her slight awkwardness when she greeted him. Probably it passed unnoticed anyway, because her mother had a great deal to say and he spent several minutes talking to Nanny. When he eventually asked her how her foot was progressing, she had got over the awkwardness and answered him in her usual calm manner, telling him that it was giving no trouble at all.

'In that case, come along to the treatment room and we'll get Monique to take out alternate stitches,' he advised her.

She stomped along beside him, arranged her foot for his close inspection and then stayed quiet while Monique got busy with her scissors and forceps. There were quite a few stitches; he had made a horseshoe incision in the front of her foot so that he could get at the crushed bones, and then had tidily sewn it back into place again with small neat stitches. Her foot felt much better even with only half of them out, and the promise that the rest of them should come out on the following day was cheering news—it was just a question of time now, before the pins were removed and, finally, the plaster. She shut her eyes, picturing Leslie's face when she ran to meet him.

Mr Bamstra didn't stay long after that; just long enough for her mother and Nanny to make their protracted good nights before he ushered them out of the room, and this time he didn't come back. Esmeralda, her head full of Leslie and the visit he must surely pay any day now, hardly noticed him go.

The following afternoon her mother and Nanny went back to England, and it wasn't until they had gone, leaving enough flowers, books and chocolates to stock a shop, that she remembered that neither of them had told her a word about Mr Bamstra's home, or indeed, anything about him at all. She recollected that she had asked her mother what his house was like, and that lady had said vaguely that it was very nice before Nanny had interrupted with something or other, and somehow, each time she had meant to bring the subject up, she had been hedged off. A pity, she thought, having another go at the despised knitting. She should have made more of a thing of it, but her head had been, and still was, filled with thoughts of Leslie. She had talked about him quite a bit to her mother, happy to be able to do so, and not noticing that her mother's replies had been a little cool, and now that she was alone she occupied herself once more with making excuses for him. The urge to write to him—even to telephone—was very great, but she had enough sense not to do that, and there could be a dozen reasons why he hadn't come—perhaps he was waiting until the plaster was off. That was weeks away, she reminded herself gloomily.

The days passed slowly, and on each one of them Esmeralda looked for the post and was disappointed. She became a little peevish, lost her appetite and was discovered, far too frequently, wide awake at night when she should have been sleeping. It was a week before she saw Mr Bamstra again, and when he did come, looking remote in his white coat, and with Octavius and Monique in attendance, she wished him good morning quite snappishly. 'You don't come very often, do you?' she added rudely.

He chose to ignore her ill manners. 'I've been in Vienna,' he told her pleasantly. 'How's the foot?'

'Quite all right, thank you. How much longer...'

'Getting fed up with it? Not much longer now—you're doing your exercises?' And when she nodded: 'And now tell me why you are sleeping badly, eating badly and finding life generally unpleasant.'

She turned a pair of stormy eyes on his. 'I've been

beastly to everyone, haven't I? I don't blame them for complaining.'

'No one has complained, Esmeralda, and you haven't been beastly—and will you answer my question?'

She was still looking at him. Suddenly she gave a sniff and burst into tears—something which she realized she had been longing to do for days now. The relief was so great that she really let herself go, the tears streaming down her cheeks, while sobs, snorts and sniffs followed each other in a rush.

Mr Bamstra eyed her thoughtfully and without surprise, nodded to his two companions and then closed the door soundlessly behind them, then he went and sat down on the side of the bed, his large hands clasped between his knees, apparently studying the floor. He waited with patience while she sniffed and snorted and sobbed herself to a standstill before saying in a kindly voice: 'Wash your face, there's a good girl, and then tell me all about it.' And such was the gentleness of his voice that Esmeralda did as she was told without even bothering to look at her hideously reddened and puffy face, and then went and sat down again.

'Leslie?' asked Mr Bamstra with an impersonal sympathy which somehow compelled her to answer him.

She nodded, and without any further prompting

poured it all out in a toneless voice which seemed somehow worse than her outburst of tears had been.

'Only a telegram,' she uttered. 'I've been here ages, haven't I? And I've been making all kinds of excuses, but it's no good any more, he's n-not coming—I don't suppose he ever will—perhaps he never meant to, but why did he say…?' She stopped and took a deep breath. 'He took me home for the weekend, you know, and I thought…' She gulped. 'I don't really care about my beastly foot any more,' she declared furiously. 'I know I sound ungrateful and stupid, but I don't—it just d-doesn't matter—for all I care you can take the wretched pins out now and hack off the plaster and I'll be a cripple again!'

Mr Bamstra made no reply to this impassioned, un-balanced speech, so in the end she was forced to look at him. He had continued the study of the floor while she had been speaking, but now he looked up.

'There are a number of things I could suggest,' he remarked mildly. 'You could telephone him at Trent's—but that's out, isn't it? You're not that kind of a girl; you would rather live your life out in sorrow than drop your guard, wouldn't you? You could tele-phone your friends—and you must have any number of them at the hospital—and ask a few questions, but that smacks of a lack of trust, doesn't it? That won't do either.' His grey eyes held hers. 'And you could wait just a little longer—three days, perhaps?'

He unclasped his hands and removed a tiny thread

from his exquisitely cut trousers. 'Personally, I am a firm believer in miracles.'

Esmeralda's eyes shone with green fire between their puffy lids. 'Would you do that, Mr Bamstra? Truly?'

'Truly I would, Esmeralda.' He got to his feet. 'I shall take those pins out in one week's time. In a way, your foot is a small miracle, isn't it?'

Her poor blotchy face went red. 'I'm sorry I said that, it was rotten of me. You see, I'm not a very nice person when things go wrong, am I?'

He stood looking down at her, smiling faintly. 'You must remember, Esmeralda, that to the people who love you, you are always a very nice person—tears and temper and rude words just don't matter to them, because they love you and understand.'

Presently he went away, and she went to the mirror and did things to her face, feeling better than she had done for days. Mr Bamstra had sounded so very sure, and somehow he had made her feel sure too. She would do exactly as he had suggested and wait for several days—three days. Probably she had got het up about nothing at all; an overworked imagination had made her see everything with exaggerated despondency. Buoyed up with these thoughts, she went for a walk along the corridor and into the lift foyer, exchanged the time of day with one or two other patients and walked carefully back again, and Monique, meeting her on the way, stopped for a friendly chat without mentioning once that Esmeralda had been in floods of tears not half an hour earlier.

She didn't see Mr Bamstra at all the next day, nor on the two days which followed it, and although she was vaguely regretful about it, she didn't allow it to spoil her days. She presented a cheerful face to the world, excelled herself at physio and wrote a number of long, chatty letters, and for good measure ate all her meals in an exemplary manner.

It was on the morning of the following day that she glanced up as she was mounting the stairs from Physio and saw Leslie watching her from the top. Her first thought was that Mr Bamstra had been right, the second, that Leslie wasn't smiling. But even as she was thinking it, the charmingly boyish grin which made him so attractive broke over his face. Esmeralda forced herself to climb the remaining stairs at a reasonable pace, half expecting him to come and meet her half way, but he stayed where he was. Only when she had reached his side did he say: 'Hullo, there— I've been waiting quite ten minutes.'

Esmeralda stifled a wish to tell him that she had been waiting for him for a good deal longer than that. Instead she smiled and said in a carefully friendly voice: 'I was in Physio—I go twice a day.'

She began to walk down the corridor towards her room. 'I'm sorry if you had to wait—will you stay for coffee?' She smiled brightly as she spoke. Something wasn't right—she had been so happy when she had seen him there, waiting for her, but now she wasn't so sure. Perhaps he felt awkward at meeting her again, or because he hadn't written. She went on: 'Thanks for the telegram.'

For a moment he looked as though he had no idea what she was talking about. 'Oh, the telegram—we've been busy. This is a nice room, they've done you proud.'

She sat down by the open window and waved him to the other chair. 'They're all very kind and the nurses are dears.'

Esmeralda had tucked her foot under the long full skirt of her robe; surely he was going to ask her about it? But instead, there was an awkward pause so that she felt forced to relieve the constraint between them with small talk. Only when she at length came to a standstill did Leslie ask reluctantly: 'Well, how's this marvellous foot?'

'Super!' She hadn't meant to sound so eager, but she hadn't been able to help herself. She thrust the awkward plastered thing out for his inspection. It was discoloured still, the scar showed red and raw and the pins stuck out from the tops of her toes like nightmare nails; not a nice sight, but not an unusual one for an orthopaedic surgeon to see, so that his: 'Good God, what a filthy mess!' shook her mightily.

'The pins are coming out in three days,' she offered, 'and it's been a great success. When the plaster's off I'll be able to walk and run and dance...'

'I wouldn't count on that,' Leslie said lightly, and got up. 'Well, I must be off, Esmeralda.'

She stared at him, astonished, not believing her ears. 'Back to Trent's? But you've only just got here—did you come for the day? But surely...?'

She was interrupted by the opening of the door and the entry of a tall, good-looking girl in a floor-length cotton dress, rows of beads and a preposterous leather hat a-top dark flowing hair. This vision glanced at her, smiled perfunctorily and remarked: 'Oh, there you are, darling—no, it's no use you looking at me like a thundercloud. You said fifteen minutes at the most, and it's more than half an hour—I got bored.'

She transferred her dark eyes to Esmeralda's amazed face. 'Hullo, you must be Esmeralda.' She glanced down at the plastered foot and shuddered. 'You're a cripple, aren't you? I'm so sorry, it must be a dead bore for you—Leslie's sorry for you too.'

She might have gone on at some length, oblivious of Leslie's fury and Esmeralda's white face, only Mr Bamstra, appearing apparently from thin air, eased his large frame past her, took the door handle from her grasp, and opened the door wide.

'I really think that you should go,' he said in a harsh voice quite unlike his usual placid tones. 'And as for you...' The harshness had become a growl as he turned a quelling gaze upon Leslie. 'Out,' said Mr Bamstra very softly.

He was breathing rather fast, but his face was impassive, although he added something in his own language, which, while unintelligible to his listeners, left no doubt as to his feelings and caused them to leave with almost undignified haste. He shut the door behind them, picked up the flowers which Leslie had brought with him, pitched them carelessly over the balcony into the courtyard below and sat down where he usually did, on the side of the bed.

Esmeralda had the sensation that she was having a particularly nasty dream—indeed, she wished that were so, for one woke up from dreams, and she was unfortunately very much awake. Without looking at her companion she spoke at length. 'That was his girl-friend,' she mumbled, thinking her sad thoughts aloud. 'She's very pretty. She called me a cripple. And Leslie—I wonder why he came. He doesn't love me, you know—I'm not even sure that he likes me. He looked at my foot as though it was something b-beastly.' She gave a long sigh. 'I did think that he liked me,' she reiterated. 'He took me out and drove me home for that weekend. Do you suppose he only wanted my money? I didn't think he knew about it, but perhaps he did—it's not a great fortune but enough to set up a practice...' She sighed again and asked in a polite voice: 'Would you like a cup of tea, Mr Bamstra?'

She looked at him then and managed a small smile which trembled and died almost at once. 'I was looking forward to Leslie coming—you see, I was sure he would because you had said so, and when I saw him I remembered what you'd said about a miracle and waiting three days...'

He was looking at her steadily and something in his face gave her pause. 'Oh—you knew that he was coming,' and then: 'You asked him to come.'

He nodded, unsmiling. 'Yes, I did, Esmeralda.'

She exclaimed childishly: 'Oh, why did you do that—it wasn't a miracle.'

'Yes, it was—at least it was to start with. You see, you needed one very badly, didn't you? You have been in an apathetic doldrum for several days, haven't you, and that seemed the best way of getting you out of it.'

'You're angry, aren't you?'

'Yes—not with you. I didn't imagine for one moment that you would be subjected to such callous treatment, but I had no idea that Chapman was going to bring that girl with him.'

She asked with the wisdom of hindsight: 'You've known all along that he didn't care tuppence for me, haven't you, so why did you ask him to come?'

'Because I could have been mistaken, and he had to have his chance—you couldn't have gone on expecting a letter or a visit for ever, could you? And there could have been a valid reason for his not writing or coming. I wondered when I telephoned to let him know that the operation had been a success…and when he didn't write, I asked him to write to you; that a letter would encourage you. You had a telegram instead, so when I was at Trent's I saw him and suggested that he might like to come over and see you. I knew then about this girl, but she might not have been important—as I told you, I had no idea that she would be with him.'

'You were so sure that he didn't love me,' she said sadly.

'Oh, yes.' He smiled faintly. 'If he had loved you, my dear, he would have been here, making sure that I did everything properly in theatre, visiting you every hour of the day, watching every procedure with a hawk eye, filling your room with flowers…'

Esmeralda suspected that under his elegant, placid appearance, Mr Bamstra was a romantic, but at, present her poor head was too full of her own miseries to give much thought to that. 'He was busy,' she said feebly.

'Don't give me that,' said her companion unexpectedly and with some force, so that she looked at him again with amazement; it seemed to her to be exquisitely funny that he should use such an inelegant phrase. She laughed, and the laughter turned quite unexpectedly to heartfelt sobs.

'Oh, what shall I do?' she wailed, and found herself

plucked from her chair and engulfed in a soothing, impersonal embrace.

'That's better,' observed Mr Bamstra, addressing no one in particular, 'I don't hold with all this dry-eyed courage—though mind you,' he rambled on in a comfortable way, 'you've become quite a watering pot, haven't you? Whenever I come—the nurses will think that I beat you.'

The idea was so ludicrous that she stopped sobbing to giggle, heaved a watery sigh and said: 'Thank you for being such a dear, Mr Bamstra. I'll feel better about it presently; just at the moment it's like a nightmare.'

'One wakes up. You will promise me something, Esmeralda.'

'I don't know—if I can, I will.'

'I shall write you up for something to make you sleep soundly all night—you will oblige me by taking it.'

'I never take sleeping pills,' she protested.

'I know, that's why I must have your promise—I wouldn't ask you to take one if I didn't think it was a good idea.'

A wave of remembered unhappiness washed over her. She blinked back threatening tears and said again: 'You're so kind, Mr Bamstra.'

'Try calling me Thimo.' His tone was avuncular, but there was a gleam in his eyes which made nonsense of that.

CHAPTER SIX

ESMERALDA had thought that she would never sleep that night, and when *Nacht Zuster,* on her first round of the evening, stood over her while she swallowed the tablets Mr Bamstra had prescribed for her, she was quite sure that it would be impossible for her to close her eyes, let alone sleep.

The day had been long. Mr Bamstra had remained to drink a cup of tea with her, but that had been barely midday; the afternoon and evening had stretched endlessly after that, even though Monique had spent a good part of her mealtime with her, and Octavius had come just before tea, ostensibly to arrange for the removal of the pins. He had sat talking to her for a little while, obviously intent on cheering her up, for he had told her a number of long-winded jokes, given her a précis of Leiden's history, and then asked her, in a round-about way, if she liked Monique.

'She's smashing,' Esmeralda had said, 'quite one of the prettiest girls I've ever met, and a splendid nurse.'

Octavius had beamed at her. 'I like her also—this evening we visit the cinema together.'

'That'll be jolly.' Esmeralda, determined to forget

her own miseries as much as possible and be interested in someone else, went on: 'How often do you
get a free evening?'

'Twice—sometimes three times in each week. I
share them with the two orthopaedic housemen, but
sometimes there is an emergency and then we get
none at all.'

'And then Mr Bamstra comes in?'

'Of course. He is in Utrecht now; he was late leaving here and so his list was put back. He will be
operating until quite late this evening, I think, and
tomorrow he has a heavy list for the afternoon.'

He had gone soon after that, leaving her to wonder
if it was because of her that Mr Bamstra had been
delayed.

She lay thinking about it now, her eyes wide open
and sleep quite impossible. She was going to have a
wakeful night despite Mr Bamstra's pills. In a way it
was a good thing, for it would give her a chance to
think about her future; one always thought clearly in
the dead of night.

She woke to find the sun streaming in through the
window and Anna standing by her bed with the thermometer in one hand and the tea tray in the other.
Esmeralda sat up and said good morning in a be-
mused way, took the thermometer and stuck it under
her tongue and perched the tray on her knees, then
she took the thermometer out again almost at once to

exclaim: 'But I don't even remember feeling sleepy.
I'd never felt more wide awake—I didn't wake once.'

Anna grinned. 'Mr Bamstra does not make mistakes about these things,' she pointed out. 'He wished
you to sleep and you have done so. He came at one
o'clock this morning and was satisfied.'

Esmeralda poured her tea. 'Did I snore?' she asked
anxiously.

'No, you slept, that was all.'

Esmeralda put the thermometer back in her mouth.
A night's sleep had worked wonders. She was unhappy, and she would be that for some time to come,
but she wasn't going to be silly about it again. Leslie
would be locked away in the back of her mind, and
although she might never forget him, she would at
least learn to forget the future she had painted for
herself. She examined the thermometer, said 'Normal,' and poured her tea as she enquired as to what
sort of night Anna had had, and then listened with
apparent interest in her answers, fighting off the awful
feeling that nothing mattered any more.

She got the better of it presently and went through
her normal routine after breakfast, then settled down
to work at some charming embroidery her mother had
brought for her to do—little Dutch figures, windmills
and houses arranged down the length of an old-
fashioned bell-pull. Mrs Jones had declared that it was
something she had wanted to possess all her life and
Esmeralda, threading her needle, vowed silently to

have it finished before she went back home. It would give her an aim in life at present she felt that she had none.

She was stitching away laboriously when Mr Bamstra came in. He greeted her affably, observed that he was glad to hear from Monique that she had had a good night, and added: 'You look nice sitting there with your needlework—I don't think knitting suits you.'

She had to laugh at little at that. 'I don't think it does either—I don't intend to do any more, much prefer this.'

'What were you knitting?'

She supposed that it was inevitable that he should ask that. She said in a colourless voice: 'It was going to be a pullover.'

He gave her a quick look from under his lids and said easily: 'Turn it into a cardigan for Nanny's Christmas present—or make me some gloves for when I take the dogs out in the winter.'

She seized on that, happy to escape her thoughts. Dogs? How many?'

'Two—a bassett hound and an animal of no known origin.'

'You find time to take them out every day?'

'Almost always.'

'Mother told me that you had a nice house,' she ventured.

He smiled pleasantly, 'That was kind of her,' and

added disappointingly: 'About these pins—I'll have them out the day after tomorrow—nine o'clock sharp, and the day after that I've promised Loveday that I would drive you up to stay with them, if you would like that.'

'Oh, very much—how kind of her, and you, to me, but isn't it encroaching on your time?'

'No.' He sounded matter-of-fact. 'I intended going up to Friesland in any case. Toukje gets fretful if I don't go as often as I can.'

He glanced at his watch and walked to the door. 'My list is starting early,' he told her, and went, leaving her feeling mildly frustrated, for she had been on the point of framing a discreet question or two about Toukje.

She didn't see him again until she walked into the smaller of the two theatres with Monique, to be helped on to the table, told to make herself comfortable and keep still.

'This won't hurt,' Mr Bamstra reassured her, 'although it may feel a little uncomfortable. Octavius, be good enough to hold the leg steady, and Monique, will you put a dressing towel just here?' Esmeralda had no view at all. Octavius, his back towards her, blocked it most effectively, although she could see the top of Mr Bamstra's handsome head as he bent forward to select the forceps he required. The powerful theatre lamp showed up the silver in his fair hair. He would look very distinguished when he was older, she decided, he did in fact look very distinguished now.

'Ready?' he asked casually, and gave her a lightning glance, and when she nodded, whisked out the lengths of steel with the ease of a first-class dressmaker removing pins from the finest silk, cast down his forceps, and stood aside for Monique to dab on the collodion. He did no more than nod to Esmeralda as he left the theatre, and she hadn't expected more than that. He had a list starting at nine o'clock and it was already ten minutes past that hour; she could hear the subdued, busy hum of preparation going on in the large theatre across the landing.

Octavius went too, with a smile and a nod and another, quite different smile for Monique; Esmeralda, seeing it, wondered how long it would be before their affair blossomed into an engagement. The thought brought her up sharply against her own difficult future, so that to dispel the wave of unhappiness which threatened to engulf her; she wriggled off the table and plunged into bright conversation with Monique.

She had begun, during her weeks of enforced idleness, to pick up a little Dutch. She had a dictionary and a phrase book which she tried out on the nurses whenever they had the leisure to listen to her, and although she hadn't progressed very much, she had at least learnt a smattering of words and sentences. She had a try now; perhaps Monique would be more forthcoming if she were addressed in her own tongue.

'You and Octavius,' began Esmeralda in her ramshackle Dutch, 'you're going to marry?'

She had wanted to say engaged, but she didn't know what the word was. Monique understood though, for she laughed a little and went a pretty pink as she nodded.

'When?' asked Esmeralda, carried away by her success.

The other girl shrugged, and because Esmeralda had spoken Dutch, however badly, quite forgot that she hardly understood a word of that language, and embarked on a long explanation, which meant that she had to repeat it all over again in her careful, correct English. But the conversational ice had been broken. Esmeralda, fighting loneliness, knew that she would be regarded as a friend as well as a patient from now on; it gave her a nice sense of belonging. She left the Dutch girl in her office and stumped along to her room and did her nails with great care even though there was no one to admire them; she did her face again too, then washed her hair and wrapped a towel turban-wise round her head, pleased that she had filled in her morning so successfully that it was already time for the patients' midday meal.

Only she wasn't hungry. She did her best, spreading the food round her plate and arranging the rest of it on the balcony ledge for the birds; there was plenty of time for them to eat it, for a case had gone to theatre that morning and had only just come back, so that Monique and another nurse had had to attend to him, leaving only two nurses to serve the meal.

Esmeralda put her tray down on the side table and went to the window to watch the sparrows and starlings already busy on her potatoes and chop. Her room was the last along the corridor, there was ample time before a nurse would come with her pudding and the chop was already half finished...

'How fortunate that it is I and not the nurse with your pudding,' remarked Mr Bamstra soft into her ear, so that she jumped guiltily and screeched, causing the birds to retreat to the gutter above the balcony.

'Now look what you've done,' she pointed out sharply, 'and fancy frightening me like that! I might have fallen over.' She remembered then that she was addressing an important consultant of the hospital and added hastily: 'Oh, I'm sorry—I mustn't talk to you like that, must I? I forget who you are.'

'Now, that is just about the nicest thing you have ever said to me,' observed her companion surprisingly. He eyed her turbanned head. 'Why are you wearing that thing?'

'I washed my hair.'

'Ah, yes—of course. How are the toes? Gentle movements, I hope, as I told you to do.'

She held her foot out for his inspection; it really looked quite normal again as she moved her toes carefully to and fro. 'How long before I can have the plaster off?' she wanted to know.

He looked vague and his answer was vague as well. 'Not so very long now. Hankering to go back to Trent's?'

They were leaning side by side on the little balcony's rail, and he didn't look at her.

'No!' the word exploded from her. 'I won't go back—ever.' She drew a heaving breath. 'How can I? I'd have to meet...I couldn't bear it.'

'Now, that was thoughtless of me.' Considering that thoughtlessness wasn't one of his failings, Mr Bamstra sounded very convincing. 'Of course you can't. Fortunately there is time enough to make other plans.'

He turned as the door opened, took the plate of pudding from the nurse and set it down on the table with the remark: 'Nourishing, digestible, but not exciting—you will oblige me by eating it, nonetheless.'

Esmeralda found herself spooning up the blancmange obediently, sitting in her chair again while Mr Bamstra took up his usual position on the bed.

When she had almost finished, he said quietly: 'Would it help you if I were to write to your Miss Burden and suggest that as hospital work might be too heavy for you for the next few months, I have recommended that you should look for something less strenuous?'

Esmeralda swallowed the last of her blancmange. 'Do you mean that I shan't be able to dance after all?' she demanded.

The corners of his mouth twitched, but he answered her gravely. 'Nothing of the sort. Do you really think that I would have—er—led you up the garden path, Esmeralda? I said that you would dance, and you are going to dance.'

'Oh—but where shall I…?' She paused, for really she could hardly burden Mr Bamstra with the arranging of her future.

'As I have already said, that is something which we have plenty of time to discuss.' He got up. 'Here is your tea tray, and I must go to a particularly dull luncheon—and unfortunately there will be no birds to help me out!'

Just for a little while Esmeralda wasn't unhappy, in fact she was quite enjoying herself. 'Not the feathered kind,' she said pertly, 'but there'll be no shortage of birds, I'll be bound—you'll have a lovely time.'

He grinned. 'I'll tell you tomorrow. We're leaving at ten o'clock.'

She drank her tea in an afterglow of gentle contentment, and then set about the business of packing her things, and every time her thoughts switched to Leslie, she resolutely made herself think about something else.

Later, when Anna came along to see how she was getting on, she asked if she was supposed to take everything with her, and was agreeably surprised when she was told that anything she didn't want could be left behind. 'For you will be coming back,' said

Anna. 'The plaster has to be removed and you will stay for two days perhaps—your things will be quite safe here.'

'Yes, but suppose it isn't necessary for me to stay in?' persisted Esmeralda. 'It's only a question of the plaster coming off, after all.'

'That is so, but Mr Bamstra has said that it will be easier for you if your clothes and the things you do not wish to have with you are left here.' Anna smiled. 'And so that is what will be done.'

'Well, yes, all right.' Esmeralda sat down after Anna had gone and tried to puzzle it out; she had never asked what was to happen to her after she had spent the few days with Loveday and Adam—she must have been wool-gathering not to have thought of that before. She mentioned it to her mother when she telephoned her later and was vexed when her parent told her soothingly to leave everything to Thimo.

She waited until she was in the car beside him as he drove northwards before she broached the subject. 'How long am I to stay?' she asked, not beating about the bush.

Her companion kept his eyes on the road before him. 'Loveday said something about a week or ten days—as long as you like, in fact, as long as you won't feel bored.'

'Bored? Of course not, and that's awfully kind— but suppose they get fed up with me? And where do I go after that? Home?'

'If you wish to, although you would have to come back again. But I have a suggestion to make which you might like to consider. I have a private practice in Leiden—my consulting rooms are near the hospital. I employ two nurses to help me run it; one looks after the patients, does dressings and so on, the other sits at a desk and makes appointments and answers the telephone. Willi, who has been doing that for years, is going to Australia to see her brother. She will be away for a month or six weeks and I wondered if you would care to take over her job for that time. You would be helping me if you did and it would give you something to do until the plaster is due to come off. It's not full time, of course—when I have morning lists at the hospital—I don't have patients to see, but on the other days they come between nine and twelve o'clock and if I'm overbooked, for a couple of hours in the evening.'

'I can't speak Dutch…'

'I daresay Loveday will help you there; you won't need more than a few routine phrases, you know, and the other nurse will be there to help you. Do you care to have a try?'

Her impulse was to say yes at once, for it was true, it would be just the thing to fill her days usefully until she could shed her plaster, but she was a practical girl and she could see several snags. 'I've no uniform.'

'I daresay Willi will let you borrow hers, though you will have to take tucks in it.'

'Where will I live?' she asked.

'Willi has a very small house near my rooms, she shares it with an old aunt—if you would consider moving in with Aunty?'

'It all fits in very neatly,' declared Esmeralda suspiciously.

He slowed the car and turned of the main road just south of Alkmaar. 'Yes, doesn't it?' He sounded very matter-of-fact. 'I did tell you that I was a believer in miracles?'

'Yes, but you arranged…'

He cut her short. 'If you have any doubts,' he told her smoothly, 'you can always check with Willi.'

She said contritely: 'I'm sorry, I don't know why I'm so horrid to you, Mr Bamstra, and you've been so kind.' She looked down at her plastered leg with the cotton sock pulled over the toes to keep them clean. It looked quite grotesque sticking out from under her pretty pink and white striped cotton dress.

'Call me Thimo.'

'Thimo, then, though I don't think I should.'

'You find me too elderly?' His voice was bland.

'Don't be silly, of course you're not elderly, but you are a senior consultant at the hospital and I'm your patient—besides, if I took that job…'

'Then let us compromise; call me Thimo when we are out of hospital and away from the consulting rooms.'

'Very well.' She peeped at him and found his face

as placid as usual. The job wasn't mentioned again; they stopped at a small road-side café for coffee and presently roared over the Afsluitdijk to Friesland, and Mr Bamstra talked about anything and everything under the sun without mentioning Trent's or Leslie or what she intended to do with herself in the months ahead. Despite herself Esmeralda found herself listening to his easy talk and presently taking quite a lively part in it, too so that there was no chance of gloomy thoughts.

They were welcomed with heartwarming pleasure by Loveday and Adam, and taken inside the lovely old house to drink coffee, admire the baby and finally to cluster round Esmeralda's foot, admiring, discussing and speculating. 'Very neat,' declared the Baron, looking at her with kindly eyes. 'Only another few weeks to go before you're free of this thing.' He flicked the plaster with a fingernail. 'Thimo does a nice line in these, doesn't he?'

There was a good deal of laughing and kindly joking, and a great deal of talk. They had almost finished lunch when Loveday asked casually:

'Has anyone any plans for this afternoon?'

Thimo finished the last of the delicate chocolate soufflé which she had offered her guests. 'If no one objects,' he remarked mildly, 'I thought it might be a good opportunity to run over to my place—Esmeralda could meet Toukje, you know.'

They all looked at Esmeralda, who murmured po-

litely, wondering why it was that, on the point of
having her curiosity satisfied at last, she should feel
so reluctant to meet the lady. It seemed a good moment to mention the job Mr Bamstra had offered her.
She had only just realized at that moment why he
hadn't said anything about it himself; it would have
forced her into the awkward position of refusing or
accepting then and there, and he was too kind a man
to do that. She told Loveday and Adam about it, flash-
ing him a grateful look as she did so, and ended,
rather to her own surprise: 'I'm going to have a stab
at it, too.'

Loveday's charming features arranged themselves
into a most convincing look of surprise. 'What a super
idea,' she declared. 'It'll help pass the time and save
Thimo no end of bother—but you'll stay here for at
least a week, won't you?' She threw Thimo an en-
quiring glance and avoided her husband's eye. 'What
do you say, Thimo?'

Mr Bamstra blinked rapidly. 'Er—Willi is going on
Sunday week, and as I almost never see patients on
a Saturday or Sunday unless it is something dire, there
should be no need for Esmeralda to start until Monday week. Today is Saturday,' he added gravely.

Loveday counted up on her fingers. 'Eight days,'
she declared with satisfaction. 'Do you speak any
Dutch at all, Esmeralda?'

Esmeralda creased her forehead in thought. 'About
forty words, I suppose, and a few basic sentences.'

Loveday nodded. 'The days of the week,' she decided, 'the months, the time, numbers…'

'Mr Bamstra is out?' suggested her husband.

'Mr Bamstra is in?' added Thimo helpfully.

The girls giggled and Loveday said severely: 'Be quiet, do! I'm sure Esmeralda's bright enough to pick up a few essentials. That's settled, then. Let's have coffee in the sitting room.' She led the way, her arm through Esmeralda's, and began to explain about the days of the week, followed by the two men, blandly smiling.

'Is it far to your house?' Esmeralda wanted to know, as, half an hour later, she found herself once more beside Mr Bamstra, driving along a narrow ribbon of road with a canal on one side of it for company and a pleasant vista of green fields on the other.

'Ten miles—it's on the edge of some water called the Wijde Ee—I sail a good deal.'

'I've never been much use in a boat…' She remembered something. 'Mr B… Thimo, where are your dogs?'

'At home. I usually bring them with me, but I shall be spending a good deal of time at Loveday's; it seemed best not to bring them with me.' He added carelessly: 'You must meet them some time, they're a splendid pair, although Hanna spoils them both.'

Hanna—and who was she? thought Esmeralda irritably. He was surrounded by women, she told herself with gross exaggeration. Anyway, she would soon find out about Toukje.

The road wound itself across the canal and into a small wood, crisscrossed by leafy lanes. Thimo turned down one of these and turned again, this time into a well-kept drive, nicely screened by shrubs and trees. It was short and curled round to open out on to a broad sweep before a fair-sized flat-fronted house with an elaborately gabled roof crowned by two carved swans. The house was of red brick and its paintwork was pristine; every window shone and sparkled in the sunshine. Esmeralda had the impression that someone had just that minute rushed indoors with a bucket and a scrubbing brush. She glanced at her companion and saw the look of content on his face, and at once the house was no longer strange, but a well-loved home.

Thimo had barely helped her out of the car when the front door was opened by an immensely tall, rather gaunt woman with silvery hair fastened back in a tight bun, wearing a black dress and a very white apron. She marched down to the car, talking as she came.

'Toukje,' said Mr Bamstra, his eyes twinkling, 'and speaking Fries—you will have to excuse us for a moment.'

He advanced to meet the woman, whom Esmeralda could see clearly now was elderly despite her upright walk and vigour, flung an arm round her shoulders,

and said something which made her break off and
laugh with him, then smile at Esmeralda to whom she
extended a large, bony hand and offered an unintelligible greeting.

'*Aangenaam,*' said Esmeralda in her dreadful
Dutch, not to be outdone, and Toukje smiled again, a
nice, cosy smile which reminded her forcibly of
Nanny, and not without reason, as it turned out, for
Thimo said:

'This is Toukje, my housekeeper and ex-nanny—
she almost always speaks Fries, although she speaks
Dutch too, so do your best, even if it is only a word
or two.'

He tucked a hand under each of their elbows and
they all went into the house together. It had looked
rather staid and plain from the outside, but inside it
was a different matter. There were the black and
white tiles and the plaster walls and ceiling, a fitting
background for the massive oak furniture, gleaming
with decades of polishing, which graced the large
square hall, and the sitting room was beautiful too,
with comfortable chairs and sofas dispersed among
lamp tables and wall cabinets and chests. Mr Bamstra
invited Esmeralda to sit down and said something to
Toukje before taking a seat near her.

'It isn't a bit as I imagined it,' she told him.

'Not even Toukje?' His voice was full of laughter.

She settled a fold of her dress very precisely and
then met his gaze. 'I thought—before I saw her—that

she was your wife, but I see now that I am wrong, because your real home is somewhere near Leiden, isn't it? You mentioned someone called Hanna—is she your wife?'

He sat back comfortably. 'Who told you that I was married?' he asked with interest.

Her green eyes were steady. 'Why, no one—I just supposed that you were.'

'Hanna looks after my home near Leiden. I'm not married, Esmeralda.'

She was momentarily surprised at the pleasure his remark gave her. 'And not going to be, either?' she enquired boldly.

'I must confess that I hope to marry quite soon.'

The pleasure evaporated a little. Esmeralda forced her eyes from his and fastened them on the view from one of the wide windows.

'I expect you'll like that,' she offered inanely.

Mr Bamstra's fine mouth twitched ever so slightly. 'I expect I shall,' he agreed, his voice still bland. 'I'm glad that you have decided to take that small job, by the way. We must get down to basic facts—hours and salary, mustn't we?'

'Oh, I don't want a salary—I've money enough, thank you, and Mother gave me some more when she came.'

'Quite,' his voice was noncommittal as he broke off to fondle an enormous black dog which had padded silently into the room, and stood now, wagging his tail while he fixed Esmeralda with a doubtful eye.

'This is Toukje's dog, Pim.' He spoke softly to the beast and it went to stand by her, and when she put out a hand, bowed his enormous head so that she might fondle his ears.

'As we were saying,' went on Mr Bamstra, 'it might be a little awkward if we were not quite businesslike about everything—don't you agree? I think it would be best to pay you at the normal hourly rates.' He didn't wait for her to agree to this, but went on smoothly: 'That's settled, then. Here's Toukje with a drink for us, and I daresay after that you might like a stroll round the garden? It's pleasant in the summer—then we can have tea and drive back by another road in time for dinner at Loveday's.'

It was a pleasant afternoon. Esmeralda, listening to her companion's desultory talk about nothing in particular, felt soothed and peaceful. She was given no opportunity to indulge her own thoughts either, and since their conversation was purely impersonal, Trent's, her work there—indeed, anything which might have reminded her of Leslie, was never mentioned. She pottered happily round the gardens, which were a good deal bigger than she had supposed, and then went back indoors to eat her tea with a bigger appetite than she had shown for some time. And later, back in Loveday's house, changing her dress in her pretty bedroom, she admitted to herself that although she was still unhappy, the first awful smart had dulled. She went downstairs, nicely made up and wearing a simple sage green silk dress with a floor-length skirt, determined to enjoy her evening. And she did; the dinner was delicious, and afterwards they played a rowdy game of Monopoly until Thimo declared that he would have to leave. 'And Esmeralda shall see me to the door,' he declared, 'for she hasn't walked an inch for the last two hours—she needs the exercise.'

So she tiptapped her way out of the room and across the hall beside him and went to stand in the open doorway, looking out on to the lovely summer night. 'Nice,' said Esmeralda, and sniffed with her unassuming nose. 'Roses and verbena and that white flower which scents the evening...'

'Your mother has a beautiful garden too.' Mr Bamstra was leaning against the great door, making no effort to go.

'Yes. She and Father planned it when they were first married and it's not been altered since.' There was a little silence which she felt she should fill. 'Have you a garden at your other home?' she asked politely.

'Oh, yes, though perhaps not quite as large as this one. Sometimes when I have nothing to do I poke around in it—I like planting things.' He stirred a little. 'You will be happy here for a week, Esmeralda?'

'Yes, very happy, thank you.' Her voice was over-bright and he made a small movement towards her and then stopped. 'Good,' was all he said, 'make the most of it; I shall drive you hard, you know. And that reminds me, we haven't sealed our bargain yet, have we?'

He did move this time, very quickly, to catch her close and kiss her soundly. His quiet good night floated back to her as he ran down the steps and got into his car.

CHAPTER SEVEN

WHEN Esmeralda wakened the next morning she lay in her luxurious bed contemplating the charming room around her and thinking about the previous evening and, inevitably, Mr Bamstra. The discovery that he wasn't married had been quite a shock, and really, now that she thought about it, it had been remarkably silly of her to have presumed that he was. She frowned and thumped her pillows greater comfort; perhaps it was because he had the calm, friendly air of a happily married man. Anyway, she reminded herself peevishly, why was she fussing about him and his love life? It was nothing to do with her.

She thrust aside a wish to meet the girl he was going to marry and allowed her thoughts to dwell on the more sombre prospect of her own future. Her mother had suggested that she might like to go home and stay there for a few weeks, taking her time in choosing another job, but right at the back of her own mind was the foolish desire to meet Leslie just once more—preferably at some big ball, where she would dance every dance in the daintiest of slippers, both feet as good as, if not better than any other girl's there—just so that he might see what he had missed.

She knew it was a stupid idea; he had proved himself selfish and unkind and more interested in her money than herself, but somehow the idea stuck.

She drank her morning tea, still weaving day dreams, and would probably have continued for hours in much the same vein if Loveday hadn't come in to see how she had slept. 'Breakfast in an hour,' she said cheerfully. 'Adam and I go to church, but we thought you'd rather not, and in any case Thimo will be over here by eleven—he goes to church too, but for some reason the service is an hour earlier than ours—if we're not back perhaps you'll entertain him for us.' She smiled and nodded and went away again, looking quite eye-catching with her splendid hair hanging round her shoulders.

Back in the seclusion of their bedroom she told Adam: 'She's not coming to church. I said she wouldn't like it very much—not understanding a word—and I told her Thimo would be here by eleven o'clock, but she didn't seem very interested.'

'My dear love,' said the Baron, 'put yourself in the poor girl's shoes—no, one shoe and a plaster. She's just been thrown over in a very unpleasant fashion by some type or other she thinks she is in love with, and you expect her to be head over heels in love with old Thimo.'

'He isn't old—he's just right for her.' Loveday started to brush her hair. 'Oh, Adam, wouldn't it be awful if nothing came of it?'

He took her hairbrush away from her and kissed her. 'There's something important you've overlooked,' he observed. 'Thimo, if he's made up his mind about something, will not be shaken from his purpose—and I imagine that he made up his mind some time ago, sweetheart.'

Loveday eyed him fondly. 'Oh, Adam, you're such a comfort!'

Left alone in the house, its quietness broken only by the subdued sounds coming from the kitchen, Esmeralda wandered through its rooms, looking about her, peering at portraits and examining the china and glass in the wall cabinets, but after a little while she decided to go into the garden. It was still only a little after ten o'clock, and there was plenty of time before Thimo would come. She stomped slowly round the outside of the house, then crossed the small formal garden to one side of it and then, because it looked so inviting, went through the narrow gate at its end, on to a shady path wandering off into a copse. That ended in a gate too, and she found herself on a narrow country road with trees on either side of it.

It was quiet and cool and she stood still, listening to the summer sounds around her—but there was another sound, too. She couldn't make it out at first, a small whimpering which came and went at intervals. It was difficult to discover from which direction it came, but finally she decided to the left; going slowly, she made her way along the side of the road, looking in the long grass and shrubs which bordered it. She didn't have far to go. There was a woman lying there, half hidden by trees, a young woman, grubby and badly dressed but pretty too. She appeared to be asleep and the whimpers came from the very small baby she held close to her.

'Oh, my goodness me!' exclaimed Esmeralda, and bent to take a closer look. The girl was alive and breathing, but the breaths came slow and stertorous and she was a nasty colour. 'Overdose?' Esmeralda asked herself aloud, and took a good look at the baby. It was very small, a week or two old, perhaps, no more, as grubby as its mother and judging by the weary little sounds it was making, it was desperately hungry and too weak to cry any more. Esmeralda picked it up and held it gently while she thought what would be best to do.

Should she take the baby back to the house with her and get help to the girl? But if the girl regained consciousness and discovered that her baby had gone, she might make an effort to search for it and do herself some harm. On the other hand, she was quite incapable of moving the girl and perhaps it would be better if she stayed with her and the baby until someone came along the road and she could get help. She cuddled the smelly little thing and wished worriedly that she knew enough Dutch to be of some use. She was only ten minutes' walk from the Baron's house and although Thimo was due to arrive at any moment, the chance that he would walk that way was so slight as to be hopeless, for as far as she knew, no one had seen her go into the garden.

Five minutes went by, and very slowly they went too; the girl hadn't stirred and the baby, sucking hopefully at Esmeralda's little finger, had dropped off into an uneasy doze. 'How I do wish Mr Bamstra would come with one of his miracles,' declared Esmeralda loudly.

And with all the convenience of a fairy tale's plot, she heard, at that very instant, someone whistling. The tune was 'We'll meet again,' as sure a sign from heaven as anyone could hope for, thought Esmeralda, and wasting no time, she bawled 'Thimo!' at the top of her voice. The whistling stopped and Mr Bamstra's voice, reassuringly calm, called: 'Coming!' and indeed he appeared at the gate not ten seconds later, saw her at once and strode towards her.

'That's a very small baby,' he remarked, still with calm, and bent to look at it. Thank heaven, thought Esmeralda in a flood of relief, that he wasn't one of those men who had to have everything explained first; the I's dotted, the T's crossed. 'Dehydrated,' he pronounced, and turned his attention to the girl. 'No sign of awareness?' he asked as he rolled up her eyelids.

''None—but a very slow pulse, and she's cold.'

'Possibly an overdose.' He looked at Esmeralda. 'You're not damaged at all?'

She shook her head. 'What do you want me to do?'

He leaned over and to her great surprise, kissed her cheek gently. 'What a sensible girl you are,' he remarked, and even in the anxiety of the moment, she found herself annoyed at that. There wasn't much glamour attached to being sensible, but then she wasn't glamorous…

'Give me that unhappy creature,' he went on. 'I'll go back to the house, telephone the hospital and then come back here. Will you be all right? I'll be ten minutes at the most—then I'll stay here until the ambulance comes and you can go back to the house and do whatever is most urgent for the baby. I'll find Sieska and ask her to have some boiled water with salt and sugar ready in one of little Adam's bottles. He must be kept away from this scrap—I'll warn them about that.'

He had gone, the infant in the crook of his arm.

The girl grew slowly paler and Esmeralda got down on to the grass beside her to check her breathing and her pulse. Her bare arm was still cold and clammy despite the sun's warmth, half shaded by the trees around them. Indeed, in other circumstances, it would have been a charming spot, but now, with nothing in sight and Mr Bamstra's reassuring presence no longer there, Esmeralda felt uneasy. 'He'd better be quick,' she told herself in a loud encouraging voice.

'Well, he's done his best,' stated Mr Bamstra from the hedge behind her. 'He took a short cut.' He lifted a long leg over the brambles and came to bend over the girl. 'Be off with you,' he said without looking up. 'The baby's in the downstairs cloakroom with Sieska. I've wrapped it in a towel and told her not to touch it until you get there.'

He got to his feet then and pulled her gently to hers before leaning over his patient again, and without waste of time, Esmeralda started off as fast as she could, back to the house.

The baby was very quiet; she sent Sieska to fetch the bottle and a shawl and began to peel off the heterogeneous assortment of garments covering it. They were very dirty, and when the baby's puny body was at last bared, that was even dirtier. Esmeralda tut-tutted in horror and sympathy while she cleaned him up as much as she dared, wrapped him in a towel and then the shawl which Sieska had found, and cuddled him on her lap before offering him the bottle of water. He guzzled it down with pathetic haste and then cried out for more; she was begging him to be a good patient boy when Mr Bamstra put his head round the door.

'Coping?' he wanted to know with what she considered to be heartless cheerfulness. 'The girl's in the ambulance, they're coming round to the house by road. I'll go with it to Leeuwarden and take the infant with me. Is it a boy or a girl?' He peered down at the small wailing bundle in her lap.

'A boy.' Esmeralda made a small, soft sound at the wizened face peering out from the shawl. 'A beautiful boy once he's been fed and bathed and cuddled.' She added indignantly: 'How could anyone let him get into such a state?'

'Apathy, misery, hopelessness,' said Mr Bamstra, and when she looked up at him it was to find him staring at her with an expression on his face which she had never seen before and which she certainly couldn't define—tenderness, amusement. His handsome features had resumed their normal calm before she could be sure that she had indeed seen anything at all.

'He's not awfully clean,' she warned him. 'I did the best I could, but I didn't dare do too much. He took his water beautifully—I suppose he'll go on a drip?'

Her companion received her offered bundle into the crook of his arm. 'He will. You'll let Adam and Loveday know? I'll telephone later.'

He had this annoying habit of going before she could answer him, and the questions trembling on her lips had no chance to be uttered. She heard the front door shut and the ambulance start up as she began to collect the bits and pieces which the baby had been wearing—they would have to be burnt, she decided, and she herself had better have a bath and change her dress, which, she noticed for the first time, was most regrettably stained.

And presently, when Adam and Loveday were home again, they listened to her tale without interruption, save for one or two sympathetic murmurs from Loveday, and when she had finished Adam said: 'We can only be glad that you discovered the unfortunate girl and her baby, Esmeralda. Thank you for all you have done, and so sensibly too.'

Here was another man who found her sensible, thought Esmeralda crossly, then had to smile as he added: 'Women always remember the important things like changing the baby and knowing how to stop it crying.' And Loveday chimed in with: 'And thank you for thinking about little Adam, my dear.'

The two girls smiled at each other and Esmeralda said: 'Oh, but that was Thimo—he warned everyone when he came up to the house, though I don't think the baby was ill with anything, just starved and dehydrated and fearfully dirty, but you can't be sure, can you?'

They were having drinks before lunch when Thimo telephoned. Adam went away to answer the call and returned presently to say that the mother was conscious and she and the baby were in the intensive care unit. She had been able to tell Thimo where she came from, too. She had run away from home—not married and nowhere to turn—trying to make her way to a sister living in Harlingen who she felt sure would let her live with her. 'Thimo will sort it out,' concluded Adam comfortably, and smiled at his wife. 'I'm to warn you that he doesn't expect to be back until the late afternoon at the earliest.'

'Oh, just when everything...' began Loveday, and changed rather lamely to: 'is ready for lunch.' She turned to Esmeralda and went on brightly: 'Isn't it always the way when a meal's ready to be put on the table?' And Esmeralda, conscious of a vague disappointment too, agreed, unnoticing of the wicked grin on the Baron's face.

The day passed peacefully, playing with baby Adam, strolling in the garden, having tea on the terrace. As they sat down to dinner; Loveday said with very creditable cheerfulness: 'It looks as though Thimo won't get here—he has a list in the morning, hasn't he?' She looked enquiringly at her husband, who answered placidly: 'Yes, my love, but he can always telephone.'

His wife made no reply to this, but when Esmeralda had left them for a few minutes before they settled down for their coffee, she seized the opportunity to hiss at him: 'Anyone would think that you were delighted—the whole day wasted! They could have spent it together...it's as though Fate...'

Her husband kissed her gently. 'My darling, I am not in the least delighted, only quite unworried. You talk about Fate in that tragic manner, but Thimo is quite capable of bending it to suit his own ends, you know.' He kissed her a second time and then strolled across the room to let in Digger, the elderly family dog, and when Esmeralda came into the room a few moments later, suggested that they might run through her vocabulary so that Loveday would have some idea where to begin her lessons. They were deep in this exercise when Thimo came back, walking into the room in an unhurried manner which for some reason or other ruffled Esmeralda's good humour.

'Hullo,' said Loveday. 'What about supper?'

'I had something at the hospital, but I'd love some coffee. Sorry I've been away so long.'

'Everything settled?' asked Adam.

'Yes, they're both coming along nicely.' He glanced across at Esmeralda and smiled at her. 'Did I hear you speaking Dutch as I came in?'

'You recognised it?' she asked coolly. 'Then I'm better than I thought I was.'

He stayed for barely an hour, and much of that was taken up with brisk information about her job. As he got up to go he told her: 'I'll come and fetch you next Sunday.' He raised an eyebrow at Loveday. 'That's if I may?'

'Of course you can, and you'll stay for lunch.' Loveday offered a cheek for his kiss, but he didn't kiss Esmeralda, only waved a casual hand, and she a little put out, gave him a frosty nod which brought a gleam to his eyes. She went to bed afterwards, feeling a little hurt that he hadn't told her more about the girl and her baby. After all, it was she who had found them, and she had wanted to know so much more than what he had told them, perhaps he had thought she wouldn't be interested.

She was on the edge of sleep when she realized that she hadn't given a thought to Leslie for the whole of that day.

The week passed in a succession of quiet days, broken from time to time by an outing to Sneek or Leeuwarden. The Baron she saw very little of, for although he breakfasted with them, he went immediately afterwards and seldom returned before teatime, and on the two days when he went to Leiden and Utrecht to operate, he left before Esmeralda was even out of bed, and when he returned in the evening, she found some excuse to write letters or busy herself in the garden in the cool of the evening, so that he and Loveday could have a little time together, but the long summer days were delightful in Loveday's company. She had her embroidery, baby Adam to play with, and over and above these, her daily lessons in the Dutch language. Loveday taught her well, although her own knowledge of the language was by no means faultless, but at least Esmeralda learned the basic words and phrases she was likely to need.

By the time Sunday had come round again, she felt fairly confident that she would be able to cope, provided that she wasn't rushed off her feet, and that, Loveday assured her, wasn't likely in a well-run consulting practice, and Esmeralda happily agreed, her head stuffed with useful phrases so that there was hardly room for Leslie at all.

She was sitting on the lawn at the front of the house with small Adam on a rug beside her and everyone else at church when Thimo drove up. He stopped the car close to where she was and came towards her across the velvety lawn. His hullo was as pleasant as it always was, as was his casual: 'Everyone still at church? How's baby Adam?'

'As good as gold, and such a darling.'

Mr Bamstra folded himself neatly on to the grass beside her. 'He's a splendid fellow.' He looked at her and smiled. 'That poor scrap you found has gained three pounds and doesn't seem any the worse for his unfortunate experience.'

She beamed back at him. 'Oh, I am glad—and his mother?'

'Very nearly fit and well again. They have you to thank for their lives, Esmeralda.' And when she said awkwardly: 'I didn't do anything,' he went on as though she hadn't spoken: 'Would you like to see them? We could go over directly after lunch if you would like that.'

She was conscious of a deep pleasure. 'Oh, could we? I should like that, indeed I would.'

'Good. And now, how about the foot? Pain, discomfort? Anything not as it should be?'

'I'm so used to it now that I shall feel very strange without the plaster. It doesn't hurt at all.'

'And the Dutch lessons?'

She chuckled. 'Loveday says I'm OK, but Adam laughs at my accent.'

'I'm sure it's charming. You have enjoyed your week here?'

'Very much.' She paused, then: 'Thimo, it's very kind of you to come and fetch me, but it's taken up the whole of your day. Doesn't the—the girl you're going to marry mind?'

He was lying on his back, looking at the sky. 'No—she's a very nice girl.'

'She must be. I'm sure I wouldn't like it...' She stopped, picturing herself sitting at home with her mother, while Leslie spent the day fetching a girl she didn't know from somewhere or other. She would have been put out, to say the least. Her uneasy thoughts were interrupted by her companion.

'Have you packed your things?' he wanted to know. 'Because if you have, we won't need to come back here—we'll leave after lunch and have tea at my place and drive straight back to Leiden. Do you need to go to the hospital for anything?'

'No, thank you. Willi's aunt doesn't mind me staying with her—you're sure?'

'She's very pleased, she doesn't like being alone.'

'She's expecting me today?'

'Yes, you'll have all Monday morning to settle in. I have a list in the morning which will take me until midday or thereabouts, and my first patient won't arrive at my rooms until two o'clock.' He glanced at her. 'Nervous?'

'Well, yes, just a little, but I'm glad to have something to do until my plaster's off and I can go home.'

'And then what will you do?'

'Oh, stay with Mother for a week or so and look around for another job—I thought Scotland might be nice...'

Her companion nodded understandingly. 'A long way off,' he commented. 'All the same, I hope you'll go to a dance or two before you go there.'

In a Gina Fratini dress and the most beautiful evening slippers she could find, even if they cost her entire quarterly allowance. Her green eyes shone at the prospect, but she said lightly: 'Oh, of course—and I hope you'll be the first one to dance with me.'

'I may take you up on that.' He spoke lazily as he rolled over to offer a finger for baby Adam to clutch at.

They left after a gay lunch, with an invitation to come again whenever either of them had a day or so to spare. 'And your mother,' asked Loveday as they were preparing to leave, 'is she going to telephone this evening, or did you tell her you were leaving here?'

'She knows—I told her I'd telephone her in the morning.' Esmeralda smiled at the other girl. 'Thank you both for a lovely time—it was super, you know; when you've been working in hospital you forget that people live like this.' She sounded almost wistful and Loveday made haste to say:

'It is nice to be away from the wards for a bit, isn't it? Good luck with the job, and don't let Thimo bully you.'

The afternoon was warm, and Esmeralda, looking her best in a pretty flowery voile, sat contentedly enough beside Thimo as he drove to Leeuwarden. She was going to miss Loveday and her baron—and the baby— The reflection put her in mind of the other baby they were on their way to visit. 'Where will they go when they leave hospital?' she wanted to know, following her train of thought and voicing it out loud.

Her companion slowed the car's pace and turned to look at her. 'To this sister I mentioned—she is more than willing to have them both.'

'Yes, but have they enough money?' She looked away from him and said awkwardly, 'I'd be glad to help...'

'That's kind and thoughtful of you, Esmeralda, but that's already taken care of.'

'Oh—I suppose they have Social Security here, too...'

'Er—yes.' He sent the car ahead once more and began to talk about something else, and before she had realized it they were in Leeuwarden, parking outside the modern hospital on the city's outskirts.

Mr Bamstra had been right, she would never have recognised the baby. It was astonishing what plumped-out cheeks and a clean face had done for him. He lay sleeping in his cot, looking the picture of contentment. 'And that's your doing, my dear,' said Mr Bamstra softly, leading the way to the baby's mother, still in a side ward by herself. She was sitting in a chair, and now that she was clean and properly fed too her prettiness was even more apparent. She greeted them with a timid smile, and Esmeralda saw that here was a girl who needed someone strong and kind to care for her, and she wondered again at the parents who had refused to help her. It was a relief when the sister joined them, a girl a good deal older with a kind firm face, who left no doubt in her visitors' minds that she had every intention of looking after her young sister and the baby.

They stayed for a little while and as they made their way out of the hospital, Esmeralda said: 'I liked the sister. She will take care of them, won't she? The girl needs someone...'

Mr Bamstra took her arm in a absent-minded fashion. 'Yes, she does—you saw that for yourself, didn't you? A sweet girl and pretty, but not overburdened with intelligence—far too simple, in the nice sense of that word, for this modern world, but don't worry, her sister has a good job and a nice little flat.' He smiled down at her. 'They're very grateful to you, they asked me to tell you.'

They had tea at his house, with Toukje fussing round them, delighted that they had come and still more pleased when Mr Bamstra mentioned that he would probably be there the following weekend as well. 'At least for part of it,' he explained to Esmeralda. 'I've a case to deal with on Friday afternoon, so I might as well spend the night here and go back to Leiden on Saturday.'

She said: 'Yes, of course.' His private life was really nothing to do with her; she had told herself that before—he was probably only making polite conversation. He talked of nothing much after that, but on their way back, as she saw the towers and spires of Leiden ahead of them, she asked: 'Is it far from your consulting rooms—where I am to live?'

'A few minutes' walk.' He nodded towards a narrow street lined with little old houses. 'Down there.'

Esmeralda twisted her neck in order to see it better as they went past, remarking: 'Oh—is it one-way traffic, or something?'

'No, I thought you might like supper before you meet Mevrouw Twist.' He was driving slowly now along the Breestraat—the main street—as he spoke, and in a few moments turned into an even smaller street. 'This runs parallel with the Rapenburg Canal,' he explained. 'The university buildings are behind these houses.' He drew up before a tall old house with worn steps leading to its carved oak door, and she got out, looking about her with interest.

'It doesn't look like a restaurant,' she ventured.

'Well, no—I don't think it does, either. My mother lives here.'

'Your mother?' She stared at him, her mouth a little open. 'But why...that is, do you live here too?'

'No, my mother is independent and likes living on her own; all her friends live close by and I'm not too far off.' He laughed a little. 'She often stays with me, both here and in Friesland; we're the best of friends.'

He had opened the door as he was talking, to find a staid, elderly woman awaiting for them. She smiled and murmured something and Thimo said: 'This is Corrie, my mother's constant companion for years— she cooks and housekeeps and spoils her dreadfully. Come in here.'

The hall was dark and narrow, with a lofty ceiling, but Esmeralda barely had time to notice that because he had her by the arm and had drawn her into a room on the left of them. It was rather dark here, too, with panelled walls and an elaborately plastered ceiling, but its furnishings were delightful; cushions and curtains in jewel colours, with a dark red woven carpet on the floor. The furniture was dark and solid and comfortable chairs, brocade-covered, were scattered amongst the tables and wall chests and cabinets. The lady who rose from her chair to greet them completed the pleasing picture which the room made; she was small and slight, dressed in a soft blue outfit which complemented her silver grey hair. There was no mistaking who she was; she had the same grey eyes as her son and his same slow smile.

'I shall call you Esmeralda,' she began at once as she lifted her face for her son's kiss. 'Such a pretty name and right for your eyes, of course. I expect Thimo forgot to mention me, or that I was expecting you for supper this evening, until he was on the doorstep.' She smiled at Esmeralda and took her hand. 'Come and tidy yourself, my dear. Thimo shall pour the drinks while he is waiting.'

Esmeralda had had no chance to say a word, but in any case there seemed no need, and she had been put immediately at ease by the little lady's charming welcome. She accompanied her hostess across the hall to another door which opened to reveal an elegant cloakroom. 'You don't really need to tidy anything,' confided her companion. 'I just wanted to have a good look at you, my dear. You don't mind?'

'No, not at all,' said Esmeralda, very much bewildered, and poked at her hair because she really had to do something.

'I know all about your foot,' went on the little lady. 'Thimo is so very clever, isn't he? And I heard how splendid you were with that poor young girl and her baby.'

'Well, not really.' Esmeralda felt that she was being praised for something she hadn't done. 'I only stood and shouted for help and Thimo came—he did everything, you know.'

Her hostess smiled and said merely: 'I must go and say a word to Corrie about supper. Can you find your own way back, my dear?'

Esmeralda assured her that she could, spent a few minutes prettying herself and went back to the drawing room again. Mr Bamstra was leaning against a fragile table which looked as though it might collapse at any moment, laughing down at his mother, sitting in her chair once more, but when he saw Esmeralda he went to meet her, settled her in a chair, offered her a choice of drinks and went to take his own seat in a substantial high-backed chair more worthy of his size, to begin a conversation which gave her no inkling of his personal life or tastes at all.

Only one piece of information did she glean; as they were about to go into supper, his mother remarked that Ella had telephoned and asked that he should be reminded about the following weekend. That would be the girl-friend, decided Esmeralda. So he was going to take her with him when he went to Friesland. And why not? Common sense wanted to know. What could be more natural than to take one's future wife to one's home for the weekend? She was unable to pursue this interesting titbit, though, for her hostess was telling her about the house, which, it transpired, had been in the family a very long time. Esmeralda listened attentively, making all the right remarks, her head never quite free of the unknown Ella.

They dined with some splendour, for there was a

good deal of silver and glass on the damask-covered table and the porcelain plates and dishes were exquisitely thin and delicately painted, and it was obvious that both her hostess and her son found nothing out of the ordinary in this, but then, Esmeralda reflected silently, she herself found nothing unusual about the treasures in her own home, so why should they? She settled down to enjoy the delicious meal, glad that she was wearing a pretty dress and that her foot in its clumsy plaster was safely hidden under the table.

They left as soon as they had had their coffee; Mevrouw Twist, Thimo explained, was elderly and liked to be in bed by eleven o'clock. So Esmeralda bade her hostess good night, thanked her with charm, and got back into the car. The drive was a short one and the house they stopped in front of seemed very small after the one they had just left. She got out and stood looking at it; it was old too, and gabled and spick and span as to paint, and through the spotless white net curtains she could see a room twinkling with brass, its walls almost covered with pictures of every size and a great many china plates.

Mevrouw Twist must have been waiting for them, for the door was opened before they could reach for the knocker and the old lady bade them enter with a quick flow of words which quite escaped Esmeralda.

'She says how glad she is to meet you,' translated Thimo. 'Your room is ready and she will see that you are up in good time in the morning.'

He was standing just inside the door, filling the tiny hall. 'I think you will have no difficulties. I'll see you tomorrow at half past one; Mevrouw will walk with you to show you the way.' His hand engulfed hers for a moment, large and firm and reassuring. As usual he had disappeared through the open door before she could get her mouth open. 'Not even time to say good night!' she muttered vexedly, and turned to listen painstakingly to Mevrouw Twists' anxious voice explaining about the bath.

CHAPTER EIGHT

LOOKING back over the next day, Esmeralda wondered how she had managed to get through it. The morning had been all right. She had unpacked her things in the tiny room at the back of the upstairs landing in Mevrouw Twist's house, and then, taking the old lady's advice, had gone for a cautious walk, just to get her bearings and by the time she got back it was time to have the substantial dinner her elderly companion had cooked for them both, and after that, walk in her company to the consulting rooms.

Ciska, the full-time nurse, was waiting for her and, received from Mevrouw Twist's hands with all the care accorded to a registered parcel handed over by the postman, Esmeralda was led away to the back of the dignified old house, to a small room where she was buttoned and pinned into a white uniform cap, and led carefully up a narrow carpeted stair to the waiting room.

There was no one there, and a good thing too. Esmeralda had methodically inspected her surroundings, trying not to miss any of the sound advice which Ciska was painstakingly pouring out in her fluent, heavily accented English, and had just seated herself at the desk, the plaster well out of sight, when Mr Bamstra had come in. He looked the part, she decided at once, in his well-tailored grey suit and beautifully polished shoes. She could imagine his patients, nervous about having bones re-set or re-shaped or removed, sitting in front of his massive desk in the compliance by his calm assured manner. She had wished him good afternoon in a professional voice and had been annoyed when he grinned. He crossed the room and had had his hand on the door when he had turned round and come back to ask: 'What did your mother think about it?'

'She liked the idea very much.'

'Splendid. Use the telephone here whenever you wish to get in touch with her.'

He had gone again while she was still thanking him, and she had had only a minute or so after that to wonder what Leslie would say if he could see her now, when the first patient arrived.

She hadn't done too badly; the work was largely routine and Thimo had helped her in an unobstrusive way by letting her know the essential facts about each patient before they left him, so that by the time they got to her desk, all she had to do was smile, murmur a few words, and write busily in the appointment book. The hours had flown; suddenly the waiting room had been empty and Ciska had come out of the examination room to say that the next patient wasn't booked until five o'clock, and they would all have tea. Which they did, sitting together at the desk, although Mr Bamstra excused himself after drinking his and went back to his room to get on with his notes.

And the evening had been much the same as the afternoon. Finally, when the last patient for the day had gone and Esmeralda had tidied her desk and changed into her dress again, she had been free to go. Ciska had already left, and she had hurried, fearful of keeping Mr Bamstra waiting, to lock up.

He had been standing patiently by the door and she had said a trifle breathlessly: 'I'll be quicker tomorrow,' and had almost fallen over her plaster in her efforts to get to the door and out of it. She wished him goodnight as she started off along the pavement in the direction of Mevrouw Twist's little house, but he had caught her up easily enough and taken her arm.

'You managed very well,' he commented pleasantly.

She had stood still, the better to address him. 'Thank you, but of course you and Ciska did most of the work, didn't you? You were both awfully kind and patient. And there's no need to come with me, I'm quite sure of the way, and you must have a great deal to do.'

He smiled and nodded. 'A dinner date—with someone who always understands if I'm late.'

It would be Ella again; the girl must be a saint! Esmeralda made a small cross sound and turned it into a cough, and after that there had been no need to say anything more, because they had arrived at Mevrouw Twist's front door, and she was there, waiting for them. Mr Bamstra had wished them both a good evening and walked away, presumably back to his own car.

His patients came in the morning on the next day, so that she was free after one o'clock, and this time she slipped away before Mr Bamstra had left his own room; she wasn't sure if it was quite the thing to do, but she didn't want him to feel that he had to walk her back to Mevrouw Twist just because she had a leg in plaster. She spent the afternoon writing to her mother and conversing, with the aid of a dictionary and a lot of arm-waving with Mevrouw Twist while she worked away at her embroidery, of which she was now heartily sick, and on the next day, free again in the afternoon, she had borrowed a stout stick from the lady of the house and went to look at the shops.

Loveday had told her that there were some very good antique shops to be found if one didn't mind the cobblestones of the narrow side streets. Esmeralda stumped around carefully, buying one or two trifles which she thought her mother might like to have, and then found her way back to the main street, intent on getting a cup of tea.

She was standing on the corner of Kort Rapenburg, deciding which way to go, when the Bristol slid to a halt beside her, filling the whole of the little street.

'In you get,' commanded Mr Bamstra and when she declared that she didn't want to added: 'I can't stop here, you know.'

He smiled at her then and held the door open so that really all she could do was to get in beside him. She had barely settled herself when a sudden thought struck her and she turned a horrified face to his.

'Heavens above, was I supposed to be working this afternoon?'

He laughed as he edged the big car into Rapenburg. 'No, no. I called in to see my mother and she asked me to bring you back for tea.'

'But how did you know where I was?'

'Leiden isn't a very big city,' he pointed out, 'and Mevrouw Twist told me that you had gone in search of the antique shops.'

He had turned the car into a street so narrow that the car almost touched the walls of the houses on either side of it, but it widened before long into a wider thoroughfare which Esmeralda recognised as the street in which his mother lived. He helped her out of the car and she paused to study the old house again and was reminded of something. 'When Ciska gave you a message from your mother this morning, she didn't call her Mevrouw Bamstra, but something else…I can't quite remember what.'

Her companion selected a key from the bunch in his hand and opened the street door. 'Jonkvrouw,' he told her laconically, 'but it's quite correct for you to call Mama Mevrouw.'

'What is a *Jonkvrouw?*' persisted Esmeralda.

'It's a title, and explaining it would take some time…'

They were standing in the open doorway. 'Is it because your mother is a *Jonkvrouw* that you're a *Jonkheer,* or the other way round?'

He laughed. 'Something like that—some day, when we have time on our hands, I'll explain it to you.' He ushered her across the hall and into the drawing room where his mother was waiting.

It was during tea, taken from Sèvres china and accompanied by small sugary biscuits, that Mr Bamstra asked her casually if she had any plans for the evening.

'Well, I thought I'd wrestle with that Dutch conversation book Loveday lent me.'

He looked at her gravely. 'That seems to me to be a very dull way of spending an evening. I was hoping that you would have dinner with me. You can always bring your book with you and we could discuss the knottier points of Dutch grammar.'

She felt a nice little glow of pleasure, doused almost immediately by the thought of the girl Ella. She looked at her hostess, hoping for some clue, but that little lady was smiling and placid, and for once, silent. 'Well,' said Esmeralda with a reluctance which caused a smile to tremble on Mr Bamstra's lips, 'that would be very nice.' She looked at him a little uncertainly. 'Are you sure...?' she asked.

'Quite sure. We'll go past Mevrouw Twist's house and let her know.' He got to his feet. 'I've one or two telephone calls to make—you'll excuse me for a few minutes?'

Left alone with Jonkvrouw Bamstra, Esmeralda embarked on a little chat about nothing in particular. It was only after a few minutes that she realized that her hostess had taken the conversation firmly into her own hands and that it now consisted of nicely put questions about herself. She answered guardedly, trying at the same time to avoid telling the history of her life which her companion was so intent on learning. Presently she decided to counter-attack.

'It seems strange that Thimo has never married,' she observed.

The grey eyes blinked and twinkled. Not in the least discomposed, her hostess observed gently: 'He would never marry until he was deeply in love, my dear, and he has never been that—until now, of course.' She smiled very sweetly. 'He will make a very good husband.'

Esmeralda murmured nothings while she thought about that; probably it was true. She told herself that she wasn't interested in Thimo's virtues and was relieved when the subject of their talk came back into the room.

They left shortly after, calling briefly at Mevrouw

Twist's house and then driving through the heart of
the city and on to the main road to den Haag, but just
past Voorschoten, Mr Bamstra took a narrow country
road running through wooded country.

Esmeralda looked around her. 'I thought…that is,
where are we going?'

'To my home.' They had come to a fork in the
road and he sent the Bristol smoothly to the right.

'Oh, I thought you lived much nearer to Leiden.
Mother never said…now that I come to think about
it, she didn't tell me anything—only that it was nice.'

'Well, I daresay you both had a lot to talk about,'
murmured Mr Bamstra soothingly. They were passing
through a small village now, its red-tiled roofs lighted
by the evening sun, and at its very end the same sun
shone on to a large square house which came into
their view, standing well back from the road behind
iron railings. Its windows were immense and running
across its white-painted front was a covered balcony
with a great deal of ornamental ironwork, and since
there was a stretch of water before the house, it was
reached by means of a curved bridge, also of wrought
iron. Mr Bamstra swung the car through the gates and
on to the raked gravel of the short drive and Esmeralda cried: 'Oh, do please stop a minute—it's lovely!'

She gazed her fill. 'You live here all alone?' she
wanted to know.

'Alas, yes.' He sounded meek.

'Well, you must marry very quickly and have a family.'

'I'll bear it in mind,' said her companion, still meek.

'It will take time, of course,' Esmeralda pointed out, 'but it's a house which needs children, isn't it—and a donkey or two, and dogs and cats and ducks on the water.'

'I do have ducks,' interpolated Mr Bamstra with the air of a man producing a trump card.

'Oh, good.' She smiled at him. 'Your house in Friesland is beautiful too, but this one is perfect—quiet and peaceful...'

'It won't be by the time the children and donkeys and cats and dogs are in residence.'

'Don't be silly! You know quite well what I mean.'

'Oh, yes, I do,' he assured her, and his voice was quite serious now. He started the car again and allowed it to roll to a gentle halt before his front door, a massive affair reached by a double step and embellished with a good deal of old-fashioned brasswork. Esmeralda admired it while he took the keys from his pocket and selected one. The brass work was polished to within an inch of its life, she noticed; whoever looked after Mr Bamstra and his house did it very well indeed.

No one, looking at the plain face of the house from the road, could have guessed at the splendour within. The hall had the black and white tiles which most old

Dutch houses possessed, but the walls were lined with linenfold panelling painted green, and above that there was a rich cream brocade wall hanging. The ceiling was elaborately painted with cherubs and wreaths of flowers, and its cornices were gilded, a graceful chandelier, bearing a large number of candles, hung from its centre. Against one wall was an enormous armoire, carved and inlaid, flanked by carved Italian chairs; the opposite wall held a side table in gilded wood with a gilded mirror above it. Any one of these articles of furniture were worthy of a place in a museum, guarded by red silken ropes and put on show to the public, never to be used again, but obviously their owner didn't see them in that light, for he cast his driving gloves and Esmeralda's parcels down on the side table, opened a drawer in the armoire and dropped his briefcase into it, then walked her past these priceless antiques without giving them a second glance. There were several doors opening into the hall, but he went past them all, under the arch of the graceful staircase against the further wall, and down a short passage with a door at its end.

The room they entered was at the back of the house, overlooking a garden with a lawn like green velvet flanked by rose beds and herbaceous borders showing every colour of the rainbow. The room itself was large and lighted by a number of french windows, all of which were open. Two dogs came to welcome them as they went in; a large, mild-eyed basset hound and a black and white creature with very long legs, a square head with flopping ears and a tail like a fox's brush. 'Mortimor,' said Thimo, bending to caress the hound, 'and Mutt.' He offered the other hand to the beast, who worried it gently, threshing his tail around as he did so.

Esmeralda bent to scratch their heads. 'So these are your dogs—they're nice. Have you any cats?'

'One—Grimalkin, he belongs to Hanna.'

'Your housekeeper?' she ventured.

'Yes, she'll be along presently. Sit down, or would you rather stroll round the garden?'

She elected to stroll, and they spent half an hour or so amongst the flowers, the two dogs at their heels. The gardens, though not as large as those in Friesland, were big enough to contain a tennis court and a nicely concealed swimming pool. Esmeralda stomped to its edge and looked down into the clear water. Very soon she would be able to swim again. 'How much longer?' she asked, voicing her thoughts.

'Another week or so—let me see, when did I operate? Two weeks tomorrow, to be precise.' He had come to stand beside her. 'Any plans for your future yet?' he asked softly.

She shook her head. 'No, none.'

His: 'Time enough for that,' was still soft, so that she barely heard him say it.

They went indoors presently and Hanna came to meet them. She was a middle-aged woman, rather

stout and with a round jolly face, and she gave the
strong impression that even the most extraordinary
happening couldn't shake her from habitual good humour. She beamed at them both, shook hands with
Esmeralda and addressed herself to Thimo.

'Hanna wants to know if you would like to tidy
yourself. We'll have our drinks in the drawing
room—I'll be on the lookout for you when you come
downstairs.'

She was led away by the still smiling Hanna, who
forged up the curved staircase with surprising speed
despite her bulk, guided her through a wide gallery
which half encircled the hall, and opened a door half
way down it. The room was light and charming, its
enormous window overlooking the gardens at the side
of the house. Its delicate chintz curtains matched the
bedspread, its furniture was satinwood and rosewood
of the Regency period. Esmeralda gave herself an impatient look in the shieldback mirror on the spindle-
legged table, poked at her hair in a dissatisfied fashion, found her powder compact and lipstick and
applied them, then went to look out of the window.
Mr Bamstra, the two dogs at his heels, came round
the side of the house as she stood there, and she wondered how she would have felt if it had been Leslie.

The drawing room was furnished with more antiques, beautiful pieces which integrated nicely with
the comfortable chairs set amongst their splendour.
The curtains and carpet were a soft claret and the

same tones had been used for the chair covers; it was charming on a summer evening, it would be equally charming in the depths of winter. Esmeralda took a chair by the window and sipped her sherry and listened to her companion's casual talk, feeling completely at home—indeed, she would have been quite happy if it hadn't been for persistent thoughts of Leslie. She supposed that she would think of him for a long time to come; it was a pity that they couldn't meet just once more when her foot was quite cured, so that she could kill her useless hankering once and for all. Supposing he had given up the girl? He might even have discovered that it was herself he loved after all.

She sighed, and Mr Bamstra, who had been staring at her for some moments, said briskly: 'There is a rather special patient coming to see me tomorrow. I'll tell you about her now, so that you will know what to expect…'

She listened carefully, anxious to do her job properly and please him, so that for the time being at least Leslie had to take a back seat in her mind, and he stayed there too, all through their excellent dinner of cold fish pâté, guinea fowl stuffed with foie gras, and a delicately flavoured sorbet made to a closely guarded recipe of Hanna's, for Esmeralda found her host sufficiently entertaining to absorb the whole of her attention. Besides, the wine he poured for her cast a cheerful glow over the evening; she was astonished to discover that it was almost eleven o'clock as they sat in the drawing room once more, drinking their coffee, so that she felt reluctantly forced to suggest that she should go back to Mevrouw Twist.

The evening had been all too short, she had discovered. True, she had seen a little of Thimo's house, and very fine it was. It would be pleasant to sit at the foot of his elegant table, with its expanse of white napery and glass and silver; to sit in his drawing room dispensing coffee to his guests and making conversation in faultless Dutch... She pulled herself up short, quite amazed at ever having imagined such a thing, and thanked him rather primly for her delightful evening as he drove her back to Leiden. She gave him her hand as they stood before the little house together, and thanked him once more, still prim, because the unseen Ella was very vivid in her mind's eye—what else could she be but prim in the face of the wretched girl's unshakeable confidence in Mr Bamstra? She must be a paragon of the virtues, a pearl amongst women and probably a dead bore, thought Esmeralda pettishly, as she stood in the tiny hall, listening to the Bristol's gentle, retreating purr.

But Mr Bamstra and his love life were forgotten in the morning. There was a letter from Pat, a long chatty missive, full of gossip and news about Trent's, and sandwiched in between these titbits was the brief comment that Leslie had fallen out with his girlfriend. 'I met him yesterday,' went on Pat in her large, rather childish handwriting, 'and he wanted to know all about you—when you were coming back, and when I said you weren't, he looked frightfully put out.'

Esmeralda read this sentence through several times, wondering exactly what it meant, and then went along to the consulting rooms to don her uniform and cap and take her place behind her desk, doing all these things automatically without really thinking about them because her head was full of Leslie once more. It seemed as though her wish might come true after all—that he loved her... A variety of future occasions which might arise from such a situation wove their way through her mind, and it wasn't until Ciska had been out twice to set right the mistakes she had made that she pulled herself together and got on with her work. All the same, when the last patient had gone, she fell to dreaming once more, so that when Mr Bamstra came out of his office she hardly noticed him, and when he addressed a couple of remarks to her about his patients, her replies were so dreamy that he shot a sudden sharp look at her and asked: 'On top of the world, Esmeralda?'

Somehow it didn't seem in the least strange that he should know how she felt. 'Yes, at least...yes.' Her smile was wide.

'Let me guess. Young Chapman has given up his beautiful girl-friend.'

She looked at him in amazement and with a slightly heightened colour.

'How could you possibly know?'

'I didn't—let us say that it has always been a strong possibility, and I'm good at putting two and two together. What do you intend to do about it?'

She looked at him helplessly. 'Nothing.'

He nodded. 'For the moment—but when the plaster is off, there is a great deal you can do.'

She thought this over. 'Yes, there is, isn't there?' Her eyes shone emerald. 'But Pat—my friend—told him I had left Trent's.'

He said easily: 'You have a number of friends there, haven't you?'

'Oh, yes.'

'In that case, when the time comes, something can be arranged.' He picked up his briefcase from the desk. 'I have a list this afternoon, I must be off. You know that you don't need to come in tomorrow—I shall be in Groningen, but I'm afraid I've agreed to see a patient on Saturday afternoon—the only time I could fit him in—four o'clock. Would it bother you too much to come in? Ciska has a date with her boy-friend, otherwise I would have asked her.'

'Yes, of course I'll come. Would a quarter to four be time enough?'

'Excellent, and many thanks.' His goodbye was a faint echo from the door. Really, for so large a man, he could move very fast when he wanted to.

* * *

Esmeralda spent her free day exploring Leiden, visiting the museums, staring at the old houses along Rapenburg, inspecting the Burcht fortifications and peering round the small Pilgrim Fathers House. So much sightseeing sharpened her appetite and tired her leg a little; she lunched at the Doelen on Rapenburg, then decided to look at the shops for an hour or two and then go back and wash her hair and write letters, a rather dull programme she followed to the letter, going to bed early too, something which earned the approval of Mevrouw Twist.

She went shopping with her landlady after breakfast the next morning; of mutual advantage to both of them, for she carried the basket of groceries and Mevrouw Twist explained painstakingly about prices and quantities and the best places to shop. They had coffee when they got back home and Esmeralda went into the little garden at the back and shelled peas for their dinner while the old lady got busy in the kitchen. It was pleasant in the sunshine and deliciously warm; she had intended to have a serious think about her future that morning, but she found herself lulled into a delightful blankness which was very soothing and which somehow made thinking very difficult. She took the peas in presently and stayed to help in the kitchen, making laborious conversation, so that her head was filled with Dutch words and phrases to the exclusion of everything else.

She had a key to the consulting rooms. She opened the house door and went inside and up the little staircase, changed into uniform and opened up the waiting room and Thimo's consulting room. It looked empty and she felt lonely, sitting waiting for the patient and Thimo to arrive. She had to wait ten minutes before she heard the whisper of the Bristol's tyres on the cobbles outside and a moment later his steady tread on the stairs. He paused briefly to say hullo and went straight to his room and a moment later his patient arrived; an elderly man, walking with the aid of sticks and accompanied by a weary-looking woman who might have been his daughter. Esmeralda ushered him into the consulting room and went back to her desk, where she sat drawing faces on the blotting paper, while the woman leaned back in one of the comfortable chairs with her eyes closed. The examination took some time; Esmeralda had filled one side of the blotting paper and had begun on the other before the door opened and Mr Bamstra and his patient emerged together. The woman sat up at once, but Esmeralda, rightly interpreting Mr Bamstra's glance, took charge of the patient, easing him into a chair and laying his sticks aside, while the other two went back into the consulting room.

The old man barked something at her, and Esmeralda said apologetically: 'I'm so sorry, I don't speak Dutch—only a few words.'

'Then what are you doing here?' He spoke crossly and in English.

'Helping out,' she informed him pleasantly.

'Got to have an operation—waste of time at my age.'

'Of course it's not,' she said briskly. 'Think how nice it will be to walk properly again. You're fortunate to have such a super surgeon to operate on you.'

He looked as though he would explode, but thought better of it, merely asking rudely: 'And what are you?'

'A nurse.'

'Pah! That's my coat over there, isn't it? I'll have it here.'

She fought back the desire to refuse unless he said please, but it wasn't her place to annoy Mr Bamstra's patients; she stomped across the room and put the coat beside him and found him staring at her plaster.

'Your leg's in plaster,' he observed unnecessarily.

She gave him a sunny smile. 'It is— you're not the only one with a gammy leg,' she told him cheerfully as the door opened and Mr Bamstra and the tired woman came out. The woman looked a good deal brighter now, though, probably the prospect of the irascible old man being in hospital for a week or two had cheered her up. Esmeralda helped him to his feet, put on his coat and handed him his sticks, and was quite astonished when he said gruffly: 'You're a nice young woman.' He pointed his stick at her leg. 'Hope that's a success.'

'Of course it will be,' she assured him stoutly, 'just as yours will be.'

It was Thimo who helped him downstairs and into his waiting car, and by the time he had returned, Esmeralda had cleared the desk, shut the windows, straightened the magazines and shaken up the cushions.

'Do you know who that was?' asked Thimo, sauntering back.

She gave him the briefest of glances. 'Mijnheer Smid,' she said stolidly, aware that he wasn't anything of the sort. 'That's what was in the appointment book.'

Mr Bamstra leaned against the desk, sadly muddling up the papers she had just tidied. 'Admirably discreet. He's Graaf...' he mentioned a name which she remembered reading about from time to time, 'and that was his daughter.'

'Poor soul,' said Esmeralda, and meant it. 'She was utterly downtrodden.'

'Well, she will get a few weeks' rest while her father's in hospital.' Mr Bamstra stood up, and she made haste to straighten the papers once more. 'He rather took to you—says you have a fine pair of eyes.' He grinned suddenly. 'Now do hurry up and change, for I promised Mama that I would bring you back for tea.'

Her eyes sparkled with annoyance at the arrogance of this remark. 'Just like that?'

'Just like that, Esmeralda—please.'

'Very well, but it's Saturday.'

He said with mock humility: 'We have tea on Saturdays too.'

'Well, of course you do,' she snapped, 'and that isn't what I meant.'

He didn't reply but smiled down at her so that she found herself smiling back, quite forgetting that she had been vexed at his arbitrary manner.

'You see, Esmeralda, you're a nice girl and my mother likes you—she really enjoys your company—and would it not help to pass the day? They are long, are they not?' His voice was suddenly very understanding.

She nodded. 'Only because I'm impatient now that I know that the plaster's due off,' she explained. 'Only I wouldn't like you to think that I'm having tea with your mother just to pass the time—I like her very much.'

'So do I—I'll be in the car.'

Jonkvrouw Bamstra was sitting in her drawing room, waiting for them.

'How wretched for you both having to work on a Saturday afternoon,' she exclaimed. 'I hope you're not tired, Esmeralda?' She smiled a little. 'It's no good me asking Thimo that, for he never is, you know.' She started to pour the tea and Thimo handed the fragile cups and saucers and then sat down beside her.

'Did you see Ella?' she asked her son, and when he nodded, 'You'll dine with her, of course.' She glanced at Esmeralda. 'Will you take pity on my loneliness, my dear, and spend your evening with me?'

Esmeralda was struggling with a strange feeling of annoyance because Thimo was going to spend his evening with Ella, that paragon of young women; it was beside the point that he had every right to do so if he chose and it was none of her business, anyway, but the horrid thought that he had contrived the whole thing so that his mother would have company while he made merry with his Ella crossed her mind even while she contrived to accept the invitation with every appearance of pleasure.

But even though she smiled at her hostess she wouldn't look at him—indeed, she managed to avoid meeting his eye or speaking to him directly for the remainder of his stay, which wasn't long, anyway. When he wished her goodbye as he took his leave she gave him a look like green ice and wished him goodbye on her part in such a cold manner that he raised an eyebrow and murmured: 'I'm not sure what I've done, but I beg pardon for it this very minute.'

She raised her own brows then. 'I really don't know what you're talking about,' she assured him untruthfully, and was justly rewarded by his cheerful 'Little liar.'

Left alone, the two ladies looked at each other and it was Jonkvrouw Bamstra who broke the silence.

'How annoying that Thimo should have to dine with Ella—he had absolutely no wish to do so, but after all, she is his sister, and in need of advice and support.'

'Sister?' repeated Esmeralda. 'Well, he might have... I thought—that is, although he didn't actually say—that Ella was the girl he was going to marry.'

Her companion had picked up some embroidery and was examining it carefully. 'No, my dear,' she said, and Esmeralda, her ears pricked to hear about Thimo's matrimonial plans, choked with disappointment, when that was all she said about him for the old lady went on: 'Ella is my youngest daughter— about your age, I should imagine. She is married to a man with business interests in Curaçao and he is over there now, dealing with some matter to do with these. Ella is expecting a baby very shortly and remained at their home in den Haag, and although she is a dear girl and a good wife, she has no head for even the simplest business matters, so that Thimo spends a good deal of his leisure with her, paying bills and arranging for the plumber and suchlike mundane things. It is fortunate that Huib, her husband, returns in a few days.'

Esmeralda had listened to this enlightening speech with interest. It was satisfactory to have had her curiosity assuaged, it was also satisfactory, though she wasn't sure why, to discover that Ella was Thimo's sister—but then, in that case, who was the girl? She told herself that it didn't really matter, and when her hostess invited her to tell her about her home, plunged into a description of it, a topic which lasted until they went in to dinner, and after that meal, when they had had coffee and Esmeralda declared that she should go home, she was told gently that Thimo had said that he would be back in good time to take her and that on no account was she to go back to Mevrouw Twist's alone.

'Oh, but there's no need,' cried Esmeralda. 'It's so close by and I know the way very well.'

'Yes, my dear,' said her hostess, 'but all the same, I think it would be wise to do as Thimo says.' She spoke with such firmness that Esmeralda agreed reluctantly and didn't mention it again, not even when Mr Bamstra strolled in an hour later; making her goodbyes and thanking her hostess with perfect composure and nice manners. But the moment they were out of the house, she declared crossly: 'I could have gone back quite easily alone. You're treating me like a child—I never heard such nonsense!'

She was forced to break off this heated speech while he opened the car door and helped her in, but the moment he had settled himself beside her, she began again: 'And another thing...'

'Oh, dear,' his voice was very bland, 'I have made you cross, haven't I? I'm sorry. Of course you're capable of going back on your own, but imagine my feelings if you should slip and damage that foot.'

She looked at him blankly. 'I hadn't thought of that. Am I to go home once the plaster's off?'

He was idling the Bristol along Rapenburg as they talked. ''Heavens, no—two weeks more, I think, with physio each day. You can go on working for me if you like, though I suggest that you stay in your room at the hospital—you could have a midday meal with Mevrouw Twist. You could go home the very next day,' he went on noncommittally, 'but you do want to go back ready for anything, don't you, Esmeralda?'

She turned away from her contemplation of the smooth water of the canal and the lovely old buildings bordering it. 'Yes, oh, yes. But wouldn't it save you a great deal of trouble if I were to go home and have my physio there?'

'My dear girl,' he sounded quite shocked, 'but I shall wish to see your foot each day.' His tone implied that she had been foolish to suggest such a thing, and she said meekly: 'Yes, of course, Thimo,' and held her tongue until he drew up outside Mevrouw Twist's house.

He didn't get out of the car at once, but turned to look at her and say: 'Thank you for spending the evening with Mama.' He spoke formally, and her 'Not at all,' was equally formal before she went on impetuously:

'I didn't know that Ella was your sister.'

Mr Bamstra's eyebrows lifted. 'Well,' he declared slowly, 'so that was why.'

'Why what?' she demanded.

'Er—you were a little put out, were you not, and I wondered why—now I know.' His smile was as bland as his voice.

He got out of the car then, looking pleased with himself, and thumped the brass knocker, and when Mevrouw Twist opened the door, bade both ladies a quiet good night before driving away, leaving Esmeralda to wonder what exactly she had said or done to make him look so positively smug.

CHAPTER NINE

ESMERALDA found that the days passed very slowly, and they seemed even slower by reason of Mr Bamstra's manner towards her. He was friendly enough, but remote, and he showed no disposition to pass the time of day with her. His hullos and goodbyes were brisk and matter-of-fact, and watching him going about his business at his consulting rooms, the epitome of elegant self-assurance, she found herself wondering if this was the same man who had come soft-footed to comfort her in hospital and give her good advice, arranged for her mother's visit, too, and taken the trouble to take her to stay with his friends. She might have allowed it to worry her if she had had the time, but although the days were slow-moving, they were filled too. Loveday came down to Leiden, for one thing, and took her out to lunch, and she spent another free morning with Ciska, being shown the tiny flat at the top of an old house where Ciska and her fiancé hoped to live when they married later on in the year, and the evenings were taken up by long, laborious conversations with Mevrouw Twist, who liked a bit of company at the end of the day, even if she did have to say everything twice and explain almost every other word. Esmeralda's mother telephoned too, long, chatty conversations full of plans for Esmeralda's future, not always practical but always encouraging.

Halfway through the week she received an invitation to have tea with Jonkvrouw Bamstra, but she didn't see Thimo there, for it was on an afternoon when he had a theatre list at the hospital—indeed, she hardly saw him at all and then briefly in the consulting rooms, when their conversation consisted almost entirely of matters connected with his patients. She was glad when Saturday came at last so that she might pack her things and go to the shops to buy a present for Mevrouw Twist, whose birthday it was—a set of cups and saucers, each one a different colour. It was a pity that she couldn't buy her a complete tea-set, with plates and a teapot, but no one, at least, not many people, drank more than a cup of tea in the afternoon, and that from what Esmeralda considered to be very small cups. However, the old lady was delighted with her present; Esmeralda spent a good deal of her evening sitting with her, drinking weak tea without milk and carrying on a halting but cosy gossip in her hesitant Dutch.

Mindful of her instructions to be at Monique's office by two o'clock on Sunday, Esmeralda ordered a taxi in good time, finished her packing, accompanied Mevrouw Twist to the austere little Herformde Kerk at the end of the street, and then went back to eat their light midday meal. They were washing up together in the kitchen when she heard the thump of the knocker. 'Taxi,' she said briefly to her companion, adding to herself, 'and half an hour early, too, he'll just have to wait.'

She was rehearsing what she hoped was the right thing to say as she opened the door, and afraid of forgetting what it was, burst at once into speech. '*Dag, Mijnheer—ter vroeg—ik…*' She stopped, because it wasn't the taxi-driver but Thimo, nattily dressed in slacks and a cotton sweater of great elegance.

He beamed down at her. 'Hullo—or should I say "*Dag, Juffrouw?*" and if I'm early it's because I've always believed that the early bird catches the worm—not that I have ever thought of you as a worm.'

She frowned at him. 'Don't be silly. It's very kind of you to call, but if you've come to take me to hospital, I've already ordered a taxi—he'll be here in another ten minutes or so.'

He was smiling, but something about his expression made her add hastily: 'I'm sorry, I didn't mean to be rude, but I don't want to disturb your leisure, you see.'

His eyes were very bright and he seemed on the point of saying something, but whatever it was, he changed his mind, remarking in a cool, friendly voice:

'I'm on my way to Adam and Loveday; it's no trouble to drop you off at the hospital as I pass.'

'The taxi?' asked Esmeralda, and stood aside, a little late in the day, to allow him to enter the house.

'I'll telephone and cancel it—what was the number?'

She had written it down and Mevrouw Twist, her hair tidied just so, her apron removed, bustled from the kitchen to offer help and advice, there was nothing for Esmeralda to do but go upstairs, shut her case, pick up her overnight bag, and come down again, leaving Mr Bamstra to fetch her luggage and take it out to the car while she bade Mevrouw Twist goodbye. It was a pity that he chose to stand by while she worried her way through her version of a Dutch farewell. He made no sound, but she was very well aware that he was secretly amused at her efforts. She taxed him with it once she was in the car and he was preparing to drive away. Waving and smiling to the old lady, she remarked severely: 'If you hadn't been standing there, making me nervous, I should have managed much better—my Dutch may amuse you, but what else could I have done, pray?'

The car slid slowly down the narrow street and into Rapenburg. 'My dear Esmeralda, why are the English always so self-conscious about speaking any language other than their own? I wasn't amused for the reason you suppose. You manage very well, and your accent is charming; Loveday must have worked you pretty hard while you were staying with her.'

'Oh, she did, but you see, she's English too.' An obscure remark which Mr Bamstra didn't bother to answer, instead he asked: 'Full of plans, are you? I shall want you in hospital until Tuesday, just to make sure that everything is as it should be—you will go to Physio each day at half past one, and I shall expect to see results, so mind you work hard at your exercises.' He glanced sideways at her. 'Have you told anyone?'

'You mean Leslie, don't you?' she said at once. 'No, I don't intend to, though I should so like him to see me with two feet...'

'Just to make sure?' His voice was very steady. 'Naturally. I daresay he would be bowled over. You're bound to meet him some time, you know.' He turned in at the hospital main gates and stopped before its entrance. 'He's still at Trent's, isn't he—and probably he and that beautiful girl of his have parted for ever.'

Esmeralda said slowly: 'As a matter of fact, that letter—the one I had from Pat, you remember—she seemed to think that they had split up for good.'

'Did she, indeed?' asked Mr Bamstra, looking thoughtful.

Esmeralda had been worrying a little about returning to hospital, but there had been no need; Monique was delighted to see her, so was Syja, and when Oc-

tavius came hurrying along, warned that his chief was
in the hospital, he was glad to see her too. They all
examined her foot, assured her that by that time tomorrow she would be dancing on it, and joked a little
about her expertise at getting around on her plaster,
before Monique led her away to the room she had
had previously, so smartly that beyond a quick thanks
and goodbye, she had no time to say anything at all
to Thimo, but Monique had barely left her when he
was at the door.

'Any messages?' he wanted to know.

The sight of him blotted out her sudden feeling of
loneliness. 'Please will you give Loveday my love—
and the baby and Adam, of course. I'll telephone her
tomorrow.'

He said easily. 'Why not?' He had come a little
way into the room, to stand beside her. 'Frightened,
Esmeralda?'

'Yes,' she said baldly.

'Don't be—I'm not, and I'm the one who should
be frightened, aren't I?'

She smiled, suddenly more cheerful. 'But you believe in miracles.'

'Oh, yes.' He bent and kissed her without haste.
She was still savouring the comfort of it as he walked
out without another word, shutting the door behind
him.

He wasn't in the plaster room when she entered it
the following morning, so she disposed herself on the

table, well propped up so that she would be able to
see what was going on, said her good mornings to
Monique and Octavius, exchanged lighthearted badi-
nage with Syja, and ignored the disappointment she
felt; orthopaedic surgeons had better things to do with
their time than saw off plasters. Octavius actually had
the saw in his hand, when the object of her thoughts
walked in, allowed himself to be helped out of his
jacket as he wished everyone good morning, rolled
up his shirtsleeves, and tied in a large plastic apron,
took the instrument from his registrar's hands.

'I thought you weren't coming,' exclaimed Esmeralda, never a girl to keep her thoughts to herself.
'You've a huge list this morning.'

He had the saw poised. 'You can say that again,'
he remarked cheerfully. 'This is by way of a little
light relief.'

She kept as still as a mouse while he worked and
when she felt the plaster loosen and open under his
hand, she shut her eyes, screwing them tight. She felt
her foot lifted and the plaster taken away before it
was laid gently beside its fellow.

'Open your eyes, Esmeralda,' commanded Mr
Bamstra.

Her foot looked white and somehow withered, and
the scars still showed pinkly, but over and above these
things, it was a perfect foot, nicely arched, narrow,
the toes straight. She wriggled them cautiously and
saw their movement with something like awe, then

said softly: 'Thimo, oh, Thimo!' and looked up at him with a tremulous smile, to find his eyes on her, regarding her steadily. 'Thank you—I'll never be able to thank you enough—I simply can't believe it!'

He smiled then. 'Get off there and stand on both feet, then you can believe it.'

She did as she was told, a little nervous of her foot in case the moment it touched the ground it would revert to its poor flattened former self. But it didn't, and she took two cautious steps forward to bring her to him. 'It's your foot as well as mine, if you know what I mean,' she told him seriously. 'It's like being given the most wonderful present.'

Her eyes searched his impassive, kindly face; it seemed a long way away, but then she was on her bare feet and he stood six feet four inches at least; all the same, she managed to reach up and kiss him.

'I don't suppose that's at all the right thing for me to do,' she told him, 'but I wanted to.' She looked round her and saw the smiling faces and was kissed and hugged in her turn until Mr Bamstra said quietly: 'I think there's just time for a quick look before we have to be in theatre,' and she got back on the table once more while he and Octavius prodded and poked and peered. 'An X-ray as soon as possible, I think,' suggested Mr Bamstra, 'and keep off it until we've taken a look at it, if you please—if everything is as it should be, you'll go down to Physio directly after lunch.'

He nodded in a general sort of way and hurried away, closely followed by Octavius, leaving Esmeralda to be taken back to her room, on crutches once more and not minding a bit, for she would throw them away quite soon now and walk on her beautiful new foot.

She waited until Octavius came to tell her that the X-ray was quite satisfactory before she telephoned her mother to tell her the news and listen happily to her delight and relief. 'And here's Nanny,' said Mrs Jones. 'She hates the telephone, you know that, just for once she's glad of it.'

Nanny was crying, which touched Esmeralda very much, for she had always been a solid rock they had all leaned on, and she hadn't realized just how much she had minded about her foot.

'And is that nice young man there?' Nanny wanted to know in the fierce voice she always used when she wanted to hide her deeper feelings.

'He's in theatre, Nanny—it's operating day.'

'Well, Miss Esmeralda, I hope you thanked him properly, and when you see him, you just tell him that I hope he gets everything he wants in life, for he deserves it. There's not much he wants: he's rich and clever and handsome, but what he needs is to wed with the girl of his choice.'

She said 'Yes, Nanny,' listened dutifully to a short lecture on doing exactly as she was told, exchanged a few more words with her mother, and rang off. Nanny, she reflected, was a dear old thing and had a funny way of putting things, and yet somehow, the way she had said it made one realize that Thimo deserved just that—to wed the girl of his choice.

Physio was rather painful; her foot, its bones whole once more, was nonetheless unused, and as such creaked and groaned at every movement. Quite convinced that no one knew what they were doing and that her foot would fall apart at any moment, she did her exercises, had a little heat to loosen up the joints and then went back upstairs, glad for once of her crutches and secretly relieved that she was to spend the night in the hospital. She met Syja in the corridor, who gave her a wide smile, said heartily: 'All goes well, is it not? I bring tea in one moment,' and sailed away down the corridor.

Tea would be wonderful, thought Esmeralda as she opened her door to find Jonkvrouw Bamstra sitting in the chair by the window, a great bouquet of flowers in her lap. She got up as Esmeralda went in, put the flowers on the bed and went to meet her. 'You do not mind if I come to tea?' she asked. 'Your own mother is not here to listen to your wonderful news and I hoped that I might take her place. Thimo is also so

happy—it is a great success, I hear, and I wish very
much to see the foot.'

Esmeralda cast down her crutches and put her arms
round her visitor. 'Oh, you are a darling!' she cried.
'You see, I'm so happy and excited and I'm dying to
talk about it, and here you are...' She smiled mistily.
'I'll never be able to thank Thimo properly.'

'Oh, yes, you will,' said his mother in a voice
which held no doubts on the matter. 'And now I
would like to see my son's work.'

Esmeralda sat down on the bed and lifted her gown.
The foot looked much nicer now, it had become pink
and the scars hardly showed, and it had lost its wrin-
kled look. They admired it together until the tea arrived, then they settled down to an hour of talk until
Jonkvrouw Bamstra declared that she would have to
go. And not five minutes after her departure, Loveday
telephoned to say that they had heard the good news
and what about Esmeralda coming for a day or two
before she went back to England, and hot on the heels
of this invitation came more flowers; from her mother
and Nanny and from Loveday and Adam. She fetched
some vases and busied herself arranging them, and all
the time at the back of her mind was the absurd wish
that Thimo had sent her flowers too. Absurd, of
course; if surgeons sent their patients flowers every
time they performed an operation, they would be
broke in a couple of years. All the same, the first

excitement seemed doomed to wilt under a feeling of loneliness. It was fortunate that Octavius should come in to take a quick look at her and tell her that the bones, according to the X-ray, had united perfectly; with a little care, there would be nothing to remember of the poor crushed foot it had once been.

'You are wondering how you will get to the consulting rooms, I expect,' he observed, and she said hastily that yes, she was, although she hadn't given it a thought. 'A taxi will take you each day for the first week. You will have your physio here, of course, and you will exercise yourself with care—for the second week, if all is well, you may walk, taking a stick with you.' He smiled. 'And then you will be discharged, whole.'

'Oh, isn't it fun, Octavius,' she exclaimed, and remembered his heavy day. 'You must be tired—the list's finished?'

'Yes, it was a long and heavy one. Mr Bamstra has already gone—he is a busy man, as you know. He has patients to see this evening!'

She agreed soberly; Thimo was busy. Perhaps he had asked Octavius to point that out to her, or perhaps the registrar had sensed her faint hurt because Thimo hadn't come to see her. She hoped not, reminding herself that she wasn't in the least hurt, and when Octavius left a few minutes later, she occupied herself with her exercises, read the headlines of the *Haagsche*

Post, ate her supper and presently went to bed, her hair neatly plaited and a nourishing cream, guaranteed to bring the bloom of beauty to the most obstinately plain face, carefully massaged in according to the instructions on the jar.

'Not a pretty sight,' Esmeralda told herself, examining her reflection with its well brushed head of hair disciplined into a long thick plait and a face shining with cream, 'and certainly not an evening for visitors.'

She got into bed, and since Monique and Syja had called in to say good night as they went off duty, and Anna wouldn't be along for a little while yet, she decided to continue the good work upon her person and do her nails. She arranged the little bottles, orange sticks and bits of cotton wool conveniently, and set to work. She had one hand finished and was holding it up to admire its perfection when someone tapped on the door. She called come in, pleasantly surprised that the time had gone so quickly—if this was Anna then it must be almost nine o'clock. In half an hour she could put out her light and go to sleep. It had, after all, been a long day.

She looked up and realized with a thrill of pleasure that it was going to be even longer. Thimo, bearing an ice bucket containing a foil-wrapped bottle and with two glasses in his other hand, kicked the door shut behind him and put his burden down carefully on the dressing table.

'We simply have to celebrate,' he declared, 'though it's a little late in the day, I'm afraid.' He smiled at her and the smile became questioning. 'You do feel all right, don't you?'

She had forgotten the cream and put a quick hand to her face. 'I thought I'd have a go at my face—cream and things, you know—I didn't expect anyone. I'll wipe it off…'

The smile had become gentle. 'Leave it—what's a layer of face cream between friends—though I don't like your hair dragged back like that.'

'It's cool and tidy.'

He was busy with the cork. 'Who wants to be cool and tidy when the world has become their oyster and they can buy all the pretty slippers they want?' The cork popped in a most satisfactory manner and he filled their glasses. 'The Directrice would probably throw me out if she were to walk in now,' he observed placidly, 'although I did mention that I would do my best to keep you happy—though in a purely avuncular manner, of course.'

He handed her a glass. 'To you, Esmeralda, and a wonderful future.'

She sipped. 'Oh, dear,' she said, near to tears, 'you are so kind; there are so many people who aren't kind, you know, and you've made up for them all—and now please may we drink to you and dozens and dozens more successful ops and everything you want happening…'

Not a very well thought out speech, perhaps, but she did mean every word of it; it put her in mind of Nanny's message, but somehow she felt shy about voicing it—later perhaps. 'Champagne goes to my head,' she told him.

'Good—you'll sleep well and come back to work in fine form.' He filled their glasses again. 'Have you made any plans yet?'

She shook her head, and the champagne sent delightful little bubbles round inside it. 'Only what I said—but that will have to be later.'

He spoke almost carelessly. 'I have to go over to Trent's shortly—supposing I take you back with me and drop you off at your home? You could lay your plans and take dancing lessons.' He strolled over to the window and stood looking down into the dusk-filled courtyard below.

'There's a big ball—you know the one—the combined hospitals affair. There'll be a great crush; wouldn't that be a splendid occasion in which to start? The floor will be so packed that you could try out your dancing without imagining that everyone's eyes are on you, and the moment your foot starts to ache—and I can promise you it will—I could take you home.' He turned to look at her. 'I always get a couple of tickets sent to me,' he added casually.

'It sounds absolutely super.' The champagne was pricking her nose and she felt like getting out of bed and dancing then and there, but common sense forced her to ask: 'But isn't there anyone else you'd rather take? The—the girl...'

'No.' It was so decisive an answer that it seemed best not to pursue the matter. Esmeralda took another sip of champagne and asked: 'I shall be able to dance by then?'

'Of course.' He came back to sit on the edge of the bed, his manner so casual and impersonal that it made drinking champagne with a consultant surgeon in such unlikely circumstances a perfectly natural thing to do. 'Slippers,' he mused, 'very beautiful ones, and a dress to turn all heads.'

She giggled and shook her head. 'Oh, it's so funny—I mean, just look at me now! Who is going to turn their head to look at me?'

Mr Bamstra's fine mouth settled itself into a very firm line indeed, for all the world as though he wanted to say something and had no intention of allowing himself to do so; instead he said placidly: 'They will, you know. Can you splash out on a new gown?'

She nodded. 'Easily. I've hardly touched my allowance.' Her eyes shone greenly. 'I'll get a Gina Fratini model—white silk, no, chiffon...'

'That sounds nice. Drink up your champagne and I'll leave you to dream about it. Did my mother come?'

She told him; she told him about the flowers too and the telephone calls and added contritely, her tongue tripping ever so slightly: 'You've had an awful day, Octavius told me. You must be very tired and here's me just sitting here babbling about clothes...' She put her glass down carefully. 'This champagne is very strong.'

He laughed. 'So one is led to believe. Good night, Esmeralda, I'll see you at your desk tomorrow.' He picked up the bottle and glasses and piled them neatly into the bucket, bent to kiss her shiny little face, and went away.

She listened to his quiet, unhurried tread going down the corridor until she couldn't hear it any more and closed her eyes. She was sound asleep when Anna came in ten minutes later to switch her lamp off.

At the end of the week, thinking back over the days, Esmeralda found herself with mixed feelings. It had had its good moments—buying shoes, for instance; several pairs. Pretty shoes, some of which she wouldn't be able to wear for a little while; all the same, they looked good standing at the bottom of the cupboard, and as for the rather more sensible ones she had been advised to purchase, at least they were dainty with no ugly built-up sole. And then the delight of walking properly; she wondered if anyone knew quite how much that mattered; one took one's feet for granted...

But there were moments which hadn't been so good—at the end of the day, when her foot had ached and she had worried herself almost sick wondering if something had gone wrong, only to discover in the morning that everything was just as it should be, and then Mr Bamstra's cool manner towards her. They had seemed the firmest of friends, drinking their champagne together; he had offered her a lift home and suggested that they might go to the ball together, but not another word had she heard from him, beyond 'Good morning, Esmeralda,' and 'Good afternoon, Esmeralda' and when he examined her foot, the routine enquiries as to its behaviour were those which he must have uttered a hundred times to a hundred patients. It surprised her all the more, therefore, when on the Friday evening, with the last patient gone and Ciska changing the covers on the couch in the examination room, he should come from his consulting room and stop at her desk.

'You put a call through from Loveday just now,' he remarked, as indeed she had. 'She wanted to know if you would like to go and see them this weekend. I said I would ask you. We might drive up tomorrow morning early and come back here on Saturday evening. That should give you ample time to get your things together.'

Esmeralda looked at him in utter amazement. 'Oh, I didn't know—that is, you haven't said... When are we going to England, then?'

He gave a most convincing start. 'Heavens above, did I not speak to you about it? I have a seminar on Tuesday afternoon, in London, of course—if you would care to travel with me on Monday? I will take you home, of course. I neglected to tell you about the ball, too. It's on the Saturday of next week—could you manage to—er—fit yourself out by then?'

The dimmed but ever-present vision of the perfect ball gown became suddenly very real. 'Oh, yes—I know exactly what I want.' Her eyes sparkled. 'And slippers...'

He was kind enough to give her a few seconds in which to contemplate these delights before saying briskly: 'Good, that's settled. Can you be ready by nine o'clock tomorrow? Loveday and Adam will be disappointed if you go back to England without seeing them—that is unless you had other plans?'

She shook her neat head, careful to match his casual manner with her own calm voice, although she was bursting with excitement. 'None—but I should like to say goodbye to your mother.'

'She is away staying with a sick friend, but will be back by Sunday. She expects us then.'

She had to admit that everything was falling into place, almost as though it were a well-laid plan, but that of course was nonsense. Even as she was thinking that, he dropped the last piece of the jigsaw of their plans into place by saying: 'I'll drive you up to the ball if you will give me that pleasure. And now I have an engagement.' He nodded briefly, called something to Ciska, and went away, into a life about which she knew precious little—and why, she asked herself in some astonishment, should she give a thought as to what he did in his spare time?

It was raining in the morning, a fine warm drizzle which didn't prevent Esmeralda wearing her pink slacks and the check blouse which matched them so exactly. She piled her hair high and tucked a pink bow into it, and with her raincoat over her arm and her overnight bag in her hand, went down to the front door.

The hospital was already well into its day. She slid past trolleys propelled by hurrying porters, patients in wheelchairs being pushed to or from this that or the other department; it might be Saturday for the outside world, but in hospital it was a working day, like all the others. She nodded to several nurses as she passed them, for she had a number of friends by now amongst them, but she didn't stop, for she would be back the next day to make her farewells. Besides, Thimo might be waiting.

He was, but with no sign of impatience. He enquired after her night's rest, her foot and whether she had packed her bags, and then didn't say very much, leaving her to talk if she wished to. They stopped for coffee at the same café at which they had stopped the first time he had driven her to Friesland; they even sat at the same table, so that she remarked thoughtfully: 'Isn't it strange to think that it's all over? When we were here last time I was a little scared and wondering what was going to happen, and now it's all done with.'

'And do you feel a little scared of your future now, Esmeralda?'

Of course she thought of Leslie; he seemed part and parcel of the future. 'Yes, but I won't let myself think about it yet. You're quite sure that I'll be able to dance?'

'Yes, I am. Perhaps not quite perfectly at the ball, but as I said, no one is going to notice that. By the time you meet Chapman,' he went on deliberately, 'your dancing will be perfection itself.' He smiled faintly. 'I did warn you that your foot may ache abominably?'

He turned the conversation to other topics then, and for the whole of their brief stay with Adam and Loveday, he showed no special interest in her future when it was discussed—indeed, thought Esmeralda wryly, Adam and Loveday seemed far more interested in

what she intended to do. His attitude was that of a
polite acquaintance, only showing interest because it
was the right thing to do, so that after Loveday's first
rush of questions, Esmeralda tried not to talk about
herself at all. She hadn't even mentioned the ball and
Thimo certainly hadn't—indeed, he had made only
brief mention of the fact that he was taking her back
to England. Out of sight, out of mind, she told herself
grumpily, not caring that the quotation didn't fit at
all. But it would never do to let him see that she was
put out; she chatted about everything under the sun
as they drove back to Leiden and when they arrived
at his mother's house, thanked him prettily for the
drive, enlarged on the charm of the scenery, the delightful weather and the comfort of the car. Her companion acknowledged this speech with a few gravely
appreciative words of his own as he put his key in
the door, his eyes dancing with an amusement she
didn't see, and his manner towards her remained
gravely friendly for the rest of the evening, reminding
her forcibly of an elder brother or someone equally
uninteresting. She bade her hostess goodbye with
some reluctance, for she liked the old lady very much
and doubted if she would see her again. As she kissed
the gentle face she said: 'Mother would have liked to
have met you, Mevrouw. I think you would have got
on famously.'

'We did,' said Jonkvrouw Bamstra surprisingly, 'we thoroughly enjoyed each others' company.'

Esmeralda gaped at her. 'But Mother never said...'

It was Thimo who answered easily: 'Your mother had you to worry about, I don't suppose she thought of much else.'

Esmeralda was quite prepared to get to the bottom of the matter. Her mother had had plenty of opportunity to tell her she had met Thimo's mother; she opened her mouth to say so, but before she could say anything she was swept back to hospital and told to go to bed and sleep well in preparation for their journey the next day. She thought about it for a little while before she went to sleep and came to the conclusion that as she would be seeing her mother very shortly she could ask her all the questions she had a mind to then, unless Thimo proved to be more forthcoming on their way home.

CHAPTER TEN

THEIR journey back together was altogether unexciting. Thimo, far from being forthcoming, was more like an older brother than ever, and although he looked to her comfort with flattering attention, he showed no disposition to resume their strangely close friendship when she had been in hospital as his patient. Esmeralda sighed and buried herself in her book, and when she peeped at him from time to time, it was to find him deep in notes or writing sheaves of them in his turn. Clearly he was happy in his work and didn't need her society. She looked out of the window at the calm sea and thought about the gorgeous dress she was going to buy; she would wear it at the ball and then, given the opportunity, wear it again, and on the second occasion it would be Leslie who would see it. Of course she hadn't the slightest idea how she was going to engineer such a meeting; she would have to rely on a miracle, like Thimo.

She closed her eyes and dozed then until the Hovercraft arrived at Dover and they began the last stage of their journey. The Bristol made light work of the hundred and fifty miles they had to go. Esmeralda had telephoned her mother to expect them about six

o'clock, and it wanted five minutes to that hour as
Thimo turned the car into the manor house gates.

Hours later, lying in her own bed in her own room
once more, she contemplated the evening. There had
been a tremendous welcome, of course, with her
mother weeping a little and exclaiming over her marvellous foot, and Nanny for once almost bereft of
words. They had both thanked Thimo, and he had
been charming and diffident and declared that without
his patient's cooperation he would never have suc-
ceeded, a piece of nonsense which made them all
laugh while he obligingly opened the champagne
waiting for them. He had stayed to supper too, and
although Nanny had roundly refused to sit down to
table with them, saying firmly that she knew her
place, foot or no foot, she had elected to serve the
meal herself, so that she was able to enter into any
part of the conversation which drew her particular attention.

It was late when Thimo left, refusing Mrs Jones'
invitation to spend the night, as he had arranged to
stay with Mr Peters. 'He's up until all hours,' he had
explained easily, 'and I shall get there by one
o'clock.' He had bidden them all goodbye with his
usual placid charm, reminded Esmeralda that he
would call for her on the following Saturday, got into
his car, and driven off.

'Such a nice man,' her mother had remarked as
they had gone upstairs to bed, and had looked a little

worried. 'I don't suppose that you had the opportunity to get to know each other very well, darling?'

There had been opportunity enough, but it was difficult to get to know someone who didn't want you to, anyway. Esmeralda eased her foot under the bedclothes and wondered if he had arrived safely at Mr Peters' house, and what he was going to do all the week. She knew about the seminar, but it wouldn't go on all day and every day. She turned over, pushing and tugging her pillows impatiently, annoyed that she wasn't already asleep, trying to forget that once Mr Bamstra went back to Holland, she would probably not see him again. If she had stayed at Trent's she might have done so, but she had left, hadn't she? She felt all at once lost; even thinking about Leslie didn't help very much, and it was quite some time before she fell into a troubled sleep.

She spent two days at home, being delightfully spoilt, and on the third morning got into her mother's car and drove her mother and herself up to London, where the two of them spent a delightful day choosing an extravagant but absolutely right outfit for the ball, which left her with two days in which to practise her dancing and carry out such beauty treatments as might be expected to enhance her appearance for the ball.

She was dressed and waiting when Thimo arrived on Saturday, a little nervous because she hadn't really had much time to perfect her dancing but happy and excited too, and somehow, when she saw him crossing the hall towards her, her feelings rolled themselves into one glorious upsurge of delight.

'Oh, you do look super!' she cried before he could say a word. She eyed his subdued magnificence; white tie, tails, gleaming shoes. 'What's that medal ribbon round your neck?'

He had come to a halt a few feet from her. 'That? Oh, nothing much. Now, stand still so that I can take a good look.'

She stood, feeling shy under his intent gaze, and then smiled widely at his: 'Enchanting—a fairy princess, no less. Now the feet...'

Esmeralda lifted her long wide skirts and he came a little nearer to study her satin slippers and nod his approval. 'They'll do—not too high in the heel and well cut. All the same, your foot will give you hell before the night's out.' He grinned suddenly. 'But it will be worth it.'

She agreed happily, her pleasure a little dimmed because he looked so tired—no, tired wasn't the word, preoccupied. There was something on his mind, she felt sure.

But there was no sign of that as they took their leave of her mother and Nanny, and on the drive to London he made no attempt to be serious about anything. If Esmeralda hadn't been so excited at the prospect of the evening ahead of her, she might have felt disappointment that he seemed so uninterested about her plans, but she had no intention of allowing melancholy thoughts to spoil the next few hours. So she was as gay as he was and was only shocked to sudden silence when she saw that he was threading the streets close to Trent's, and when he slowed the car and turned into the hospital forecourt, she exclaimed: 'Not here, surely?'

'Did I not tell you?' Mr Bamstra was so deeply astonished that she looked at him suspiciously.

'No, you didn't,' she began sharply, and then felt mean because the look on his face was so guiltless. 'I expect you meant to,' she conceded hastily. 'If you've been busy it could have slipped your memory quite easily.'

He agreed meekly and forbore from mentioning that he was renowned for having the memory of an elephant. He drew up exactly in front of the hospital entrance, helped her out, escorted her into the entrance hall and told her not to move from it until he returned. She stood at one of the windows, watching him park the Bristol in the space reserved for the VIPs, and admired him as he crossed the courtyard to rejoin her.

'Do you want to do things to your hair?' he enquired. 'It looks delightful to me, but women are never satisfied with their appearance.'

Esmeralda swallowed this high-handed statement about her sex and said meekly that yes, she would join him in a very few minutes. She had no intention of trailing round the ballroom with the white marabou wrap her mother had given her swathed about her person, but he couldn't be expected to know that. It took her only a moment to cast it down in the room set aside for the lady guests, and present herself once more before him. 'I'm ready,' she said rather breathlessly.

'Ah, yes—and very nice too. By the way, I should have mentioned that young Chapman is on holiday, or so I heard. I hope you aren't too disappointed.'

They were walking slowly down the wide corridor which led to the lecture hall where the ball was already in full swing. She said, too quickly: 'Oh, no—of course not. If he were here, I'd be...I might not dance as well as I should like to.'

He seemed to understand, for smiling down at her, he said: 'Well, let's put it to the test, shall we?' and took to the floor.

He was a good dancer, nothing fancy, but a kind of casual perfection which singled him out at once in the crowded room—besides, he was head and shoulders taller than any other man there. Esmeralda, nervous to begin with, began to enjoy herself. True, her foot was just a little pinched in its elegant slipper, but that was a small price to pay for the looks of admiration being cast in her direction. Her ordinary face might lack conventional beauty, but there was no denying that the Gina Fratini dress, its creamy silk gauze and lace cunningly threaded with satin ribbons which exactly matched her eyes, was drawing a good deal of attention.

She said to the broad expanse of Mr Bamstra's shirt front: 'You do dance beautifully—you won't do any complicated steps, will you?'

The shirt front bulged with his rumble of laughter. 'I don't know any.' He added thoughtfully: 'But that shouldn't worry a fairy princess.'

She looked up to smile at him, feeling really very happy and with the strange idea that if he hadn't been there, she wouldn't have felt happy at all. She dismissed it as pure nonsense and then forgot about it, because she had just seen Leslie through a gap in the dancers. He had seen her too, and the expression on his face more than made up for the weeks of clumping around in a plaster; it was a mixture of amazement, chagrin and speculation. Esmeralda gave him a gracious smile and said in a breathless whisper: 'Leslie's here—he's actually here!'

Mr Bamstra's voice was unbelieveably placid. 'Yes, I know—I saw him some minutes ago.'

'Why didn't you tell me?'

'And have you come over all self-consicous and tread on my toes?'

She giggled and then asked urgently: 'What shall I do? Oh, please, Thimo…'

His voice, way above her head, was calmly reassuring. 'He will ask you to dance, so dance, my dear—enchant him, weave a spell around him, capture his heart.' His sigh was so faint that she didn't hear it. 'You can, you know.'

She stared at the pearl studs in his shirt front. They were very plain, not very large and undoubtedly genuine; she registered the fact while she allowed his words to roll around inside her head. For some reason they made her feel sad and uncertain, and probably she would have told him so if the music hadn't come to an end just then. They stood side by side, clapping and telling each other what a good band it was, when Leslie joined them.

He ignored Mr Bamstra. 'Esmeralda,' his voice held all the delight and excitement a girl could have wished for, 'how marvellous you look! I hardly dared to speak to you, but I had to—all that nonsense...' He paused and said dramatically: 'I missed you so.'

The boyish smile was there to charm her, only she wasn't charmed; it was extraordinary, but she felt none of the feelings which she had expected to feel. Perhaps, she told herself uncertainly, she was numb with delight. She greeted him quietly and added: 'I didn't expect to see you here,' then turned round to include Mr Bamstra in the conversation and was shattered when, before she could utter another word, he excused himself with a smile and disappeared into the crowds around them. It was like having something solid and familiar against which one had always leaned removed suddenly, leaving one flat on one's back. There was nothing left to do but accept Leslie's invitation to dance.

He held her rather too closely, and Esmeralda didn't like it. He talked incessantly into her ear, a mixture of charming apology, fulsome compliments and instant plans for the future. They had circled the room twice when all at once she broke away from him, and without a word made her way to the side of the ballroom, and when he followed her, plucking at her arm to stop her, she shook him off impatiently.

'But, Esmeralda, you can't...'

'Go away, do,' she begged him vexedly, and left him standing while she threaded her way through the fringe of the dancers, looking for Thimo. And heaven knew he should have been easy enough to find; he was large enough—but she couldn't see him anywhere, and when she bumped into Mr Peters she didn't stand on ceremony with him but asked quite distractedly, 'Have you see him? Mr Bamstra? He was here a minute ago and now I've lost him—oh, you surely must know where he is?'

She clutched desperately at his sleeve and he gave her a long, thoughtful look. 'Yes,' he said without hesitation. 'I've seen him—he went through that door.' He jerked his head in the direction of an arched doorway behind them and Esmeralda found time to give him a quick, wavering smile as she darted away, out through the door into the passage beyond. It was quite empty, so was the entrance hall when she reached it, although she could see old Dent, the head porter, sitting in his little office. She ran across the polished floor, not caring about her foot, and stuck her head through the window, and he looked up at her with some impatience, for he was checking the racing results and hated to be disturbed.

'Mr Bamstra,' said Esmeralda desperately, 'have you seen him?'

He deliberated, looking at her over the tops of his glasses. 'Staff Nurse Jones—well, fancy seeing you again! Mr Bamstra? No, I can't say I've seen him.' His eyes strayed back to his paper.

'Oh, Dent, please try to remember—did he go out?'

He scratched his chin reflectively. 'Well, now—no; I'd have heard the door.'

She just stopped herself in time from wringing her hands. 'Oh, you must help,' she begged. 'Where would he go?'

And if he had gone she would never find him again, and he wouldn't come looking for her because he would suppose her to be happily reunited with the wretched Leslie. A flood of terror and misery welled up under the little bodice of her beautiful gown, spreading all over her, cutting short her breath. Supposing she never found him again?

'The consultants' room,' said Dent at last. 'Maybe he's there—it's nice and quiet after that din.' He nodded his bald head in the direction of the ballroom.

'Oh, Dent, thank you!' cried Esmeralda, and flew

across the hall and down a variety of passages and without even waiting to knock, flung open the door of the consultants' room.

It was a large, rather gloomy apartment, furnished heavily with massive armchairs and a great oblong table, ringed round with severe, high-backed chairs, the gathering place of the brains of the profession when they wished to deliberate amongst themselves.

There was only one reading lamp alight, on a small table in a further corner, and drawn up to it was an easy chair with Thimo sitting in it.

The fright and terror melted away in a great wave of relief; she shut the door with a bang. 'Thimo!' she cried loudly. 'Thimo!' and then impatiently: 'Oh, how my wretched foot aches!' She paused to kick of her slippers as she raced across the thick Turkey carpet.

The lamplight shone on his face and she could see that he was smiling. He spoke very quietly. 'Hullo, Esmeralda, I hoped you would come.'

She stood uncertainly in her pretty gown, staring at him. 'You look so tired,' she said at last.

'Waiting for you has been tiring work, my darling girl.'

She took a step nearer, everything suddenly very clear in her head. 'Thimo, I've been such a fool—it isn't Leslie at all, you know, it's you. Couldn't you have told me?' She waited for him to answer her and when he didn't, but just went on sitting there, his grey eyes intent on her face, she went on: 'You went away and I wanted you. We were dancing—Leslie and I—and suddenly I couldn't bear it any longer.' Her eyes flashed greenly in the soft light. 'Are you angry?' she asked. 'It would serve me right if you got up and walked away.' She gave a gasp as he did get up and then he laughed softly at the look of utter fright on her face.

'I'll not do that, my dearest little love,' he told her, and pulled her close, 'and when I walk away, you'll be walking with me.'

His arms tightened, sadly crushing her silk and lace, but Esmeralda couldn't have cared less about that. She lifted her face to his to be kissed and kissed again, and when she had her breath back: 'Thimo, the girl you're going to marry…'

'You, my darling.'

'But, Thimo…' She stopped there because he was kissing her again, but presently he said: 'I had to do it this way, dearest, how else would you have ever been sure? You had to discover it for yourself.'

Her eyes sparkled with tears. 'But why didn't I know? I was happy when I was with you and you were always there when I wanted you, and when you weren't I felt lonely—and all I could think about was meeting Leslie again and seeing his face while he watched me dance…'

Thimo smiled. 'Well, now you've done that,' he told her in a comforting voice.

'Yes, I have, haven't I? And it didn't mean a thing.'

She leaned up to kiss him. 'I can't think why you love me,' she observed wonderingly.

He glanced around the quiet room. 'This seems as good a time and place as any in which to tell you, but first of all, will you marry me, my love?'

Esmeralda gave a long, contented sigh, Oh, Thimo, yes—what else is there for me but to be with you?' She smiled blissfully up at him. 'And now tell me why you love me.'

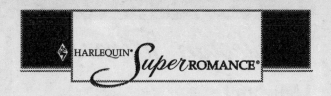

...there's more to the story!

Superromance.
A *big* satisfying read about unforgettable characters. Each month we offer *six* very different stories that range from family drama to adventure and mystery, from highly emotional stories to romantic comedies—and much more! Stories about people you'll believe in and care about. Stories too compelling to put down....

Our authors are among today's *best* romance writers. You'll find familiar names and talented newcomers. Many of them are award winners— and you'll see why!

If you want the biggest and best in romance fiction, you'll get it from Superromance!

Emotional, Exciting, Unexpected...

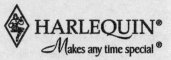

HARLEQUIN®
Makes any time special ®

HARLEQUIN®
INTRIGUE

WE'LL LEAVE YOU BREATHLESS!

If you've been looking for thrilling tales of
contemporary passion and sensuous love stories
with taut, edge-of-the-seat suspense—then
you'll love Harlequin Intrigue!

Every month, you'll meet four new heroes
who are guaranteed to make your spine tingle
and your pulse pound. With them you'll enter
into the exciting world of Harlequin Intrigue—
where your life is on the line
and so is your heart!

THAT'S INTRIGUE—
ROMANTIC SUSPENSE
AT ITS BEST!

HARLEQUIN®
Makes any time special ®

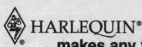